GOD ON THE WALL

GOD ON THE WALL

B. M. Spaight

THE COLLINS PRESS

Acknowledgements

Lines from 'It Wasn't the Father's Fault' reproduced here by kind
permission of Rita Ann Higgins from *Witch in the Bushes*,
Salmon Poetry (reprint 1993).
Line from 'Heredity' from *The Complete Poems* of Thomas Hardy
reproduced by kind permission of Macmillan General Books.

Published by The Collins Press, Carey's Lane, The Huguenot
Quarter, Cork 1997

Printed in Ireland by Colour Books Ltd., Dublin

Jacket design by Upper Case Ltd., Cornmarket Street, Cork

ISBN: 1-898256-23-3

I am the family face ...

Thomas Hardy

Thanks Pat

CHILDHOOD. IT'S ONLY FOR SOME.

The chosen few.

Of course, we all are children originally. What matters is how long we stay in that state, I suppose. You see, it – childhood – can end suddenly. Or, shockingly. For a few it may never be. But that's for a few, I suppose. Few.

Perhaps a lot depends on sex. Your sex: boy, girl; pink, blue.

They say boys are more affectionate than girls. Babies, that is. Baby boys are more affectionate than baby girls. So they say. Is that a male myth; a mighty male myth?

I've a boy. I guess I should say son. I've a son. Funny, that. Unmarried mothers always say that, don't they? 'I've a little girl', or 'I've a little boy'. Legitimate mothers say 'I've a daughter', or 'I've a son.' But *we* don't. Funny. Boy/girl: the possession of one. The possession of two: daughter/son. 'Possession': a funny word in that context.

Perhaps 'mother', 'father', 'daughter', 'son' are middle-class words, or worlds.

Touch. I reckon it's got to do with touch. We're all inside, they're all outside. Men always want that – touching. It's the first thing with them. To be touched. And if you don't understand that, they encourage you.

There you are, locked in a passionate embrace. Next thing, they clasp your hand, perhaps kiss it, maybe even say something, anything, even something like, 'Oh! You're so beautiful', or, 'I never knew it could be like this'. And your hand is guided to the crotch. To touch they harden as babies, boys, men: and we call it affection.

While pregnant, I wished for neither boy nor girl. I desired a sexless being. A being to be neither pitied nor despised. I could have pitied a girl. I could have despised a boy.

Leo. That's his name. Leo, the lion. Strong. I like its

sound: adult. I puzzled over the name for so long. Leo: two syllables, yet short. Too short to be shortened, or sweetened. Sweetened, like, say, Bernie for Bernard, or Betty for Elizabeth.

I am Elizabeth.

'Kitty! Kitty! Kitty!' When we want to kill the cat, eh? All those 'y/ie' endings are such a lie. Parents keeping adults babies.

I never knew my name was Elizabeth until I went to school.

'E-liz-a-beth Wallace! Are you paying attention down there?'

I live in a town. Limerick. Ireland. In a flat. Quinn Street. A terrace of red-brick homes. The Redemptorist Fathers' church is at one end of the street. The noise from the bells is disturbing. Sometimes, sweet. The Tech is at the other end; although, not really, because it is across from Quinn Street on O'Connell Avenue. The Fathers' – people seldom use the full title – is also across the road from my street, it being on Upper Henry Street. Both buildings are facing each other, Quinn Street channelling their view. Across the street from the red-brick terrace of homes are the gable-ends of two houses, one house facing onto O'Connell Avenue, the other facing Upper Henry Street. There is a barber's shop between them, between the backs of the two end houses.

That's Quinn Street. An odd street. Suddenly full. Suddenly deserted. A throng for school. A throng for mass. Except Saturday. I like the place. It is quiet. Except for the bells of the church. They practice in the evenings, the ringers do. Sometimes.

One evening on returning to my flat, just as I turned into Quinn Street from O'Connell Avenue, the bells started. An unusual volley of gongs. Peels released rapidly, suddenly, as though the bells were being tinkled by wind. Silence for a moment. Then the harmonious ringing began. Scary: being there without the throng of mass-goers. You never really notice the ringing amid the shuffling of the throng. It's there, the ringing, but it's in the background. And you expect both to be together, the peeling and the people. Without the peeling, you hear their feet, the throng shuffling, slapping along. Instinctively, I looked behind me, half-expecting to be overtaken by the throng. I smiled at the idea that it looked as though I was leading them. But the street was deserted, except for the sound of the bells.

You hear a noise, any noise, you look towards its source. I looked at the belfry as I walked along. Never noticed the building much before then. It reminded me of the trees. The trees at home. High. Silent. Violent, sometimes. A noise high up, somewhere in them, a sea sound. I miss the trees. Hazelnut. Conkers. Shelter. Climbing, of course. A swing, once. Gum on my hands from climbing evergreens. Pine cones. The fright when a wet-sodden autumn leaf clung to the back of my leg, pinned there by the wind: a giant creepy-crawly – ugh! Elms: naked columns, like the belfry. Elms: grey and dying. I never saw them with their foliage: they were dying when I was young. Crows. You don't have trees without crows. Beech: my favourite tree. They're more leafy than most. As a child I always thought of them as being more of a tree because I could see their shape more clearly, say, than a horse-chestnut, which always struck me as being all over the place when it came to shape.

What I loved most as a child was to walk through the tunnel of coolness created by the trees that arched over the road where I lived. A tunnel of coolness on a warm day: a tunnel of warmth in the cool of a summer's evening. I loved that. I miss that. I miss trees. There are none on Quinn Street. O'Connell Avenue has quite a few though. But I can't see them from my flat. I can, when I go out, but that's not the same as seeing trees from within. That's an experience. You can see wind: 'Look out and see if the wind's strong, and plait that hair of yours if 'tis. We don't want you going round looking like a straggler.' A glance through the window showed you the trees dipping and nodding, swaying wildly. And shadow. Their shadow. In the morning. At sunrise. On the wall of my bedroom. Fixed or shimmering, depending on the wind. And at night-time, too. When there was a full moon. Lulling. Like being rocked. To watch them. The trees' shadow. Especially when they swayed. Hypnotic, it was. Like looking into the fire. Or fish in a tank. In a café, once, I saw a fish tank. Watching the fish sway about reminded me there and then of the trees' shadow on my bedroom wall of a moonlit night or sun-filled dawn. Once upon a time.

There are street lights here. Their light shines now in my bedroom. But it's not the same. Nothing changes. It's the same every night. Season doesn't matter. Moon doesn't matter. The moon: a wonder each time seen. A given thing at a given time. Whirling about out there, captivating forms in its light.

Often I was lulled to sleep in my childhood bedroom with the dancing forms of the trees on the wall, the room moon-bright. Later, the shadows would creep to the room door, across the wardrobe, would dance or rest on the picture of the Blessed Virgin; these forms a series of stills on a calm, winter night.

He doesn't call me 'Mama', Leo doesn't. I never wanted him to do so. It's not that I didn't feel worthy of the title, it's just that I never wanted that name on me. It wasn't planned. It wasn't something I'd decided on before he was born. Such an idea never entered my head. It happened after he was born, when I'd returned to work.

The woman who looks after Leo had him in her arms one evening, watching my return. 'Here's Mama,' she was saying to him, directing his head in my direction, bouncing him in her arms. 'Here's Mama.' He was smiling that

4

toothless, dribbly smile of babyhood. I took him from her, smiling. I said: 'Mama?' Sounding it out. 'Don't know if I want to be called that.'

'What else would a child call its mother?'

I couldn't answer. Not immediately. Mama: me called Mama. I did not want that.

I said, 'Elizabeth.'

She said nothing. But I knew by her face that she was ... I don't know ... angry, upset. I could imagine her pitying Leo – poor Leo, an unfortunate, fatherless child, with a mother like me. I'm sure the word 'bastard' didn't enter her head. I don't know if anyone really thinks of a child in that way. Not a woman, I'm sure. Perhaps men do. I don't know.

'Love child.' Isn't that what we call our bastards?

Titles distort. Don't they? It's like you don't really see the person behind the title.

Mister. Missus. Father. Sir. Madam. Father. Mother. Dada. Mama. It's as though you're not supposed to see them. They – those with titles – remain personless. As far as a child is concerned, Mama and Dada came into this world as Mama and Dada.

Mother's maiden name?

It's something we wonder about when we first discover it, isn't it? I know I did.

Mother's maiden life.

Perhaps what I'm saying is that a thing half-named is a thing half-seen. Betty. Mama. It's one and the same thing, isn't it?

I am Elizabeth.

I am Elizabeth Wallace, and this is Leo. That's what I say when introducing us to someone, say, a new tenant in the house. I guess they generally think I'm down-playing my status.

My flat is large. It is the basement of the house. I've access to the back yard. Leo plays there. The back windows look out onto the yard, while the front ones are just below the level of the lawn. The daffodils bob down at me in the springtime: a strange view of a daffodil. The steps up to the front door are just to the right of my sitting-room window. I have two bedrooms, a sitting-room and kitchen. I share the bathroom, which is two floors above.

I was in no rush when choosing this flat. It was calmly done, like all things planned and considered. I'd been to see a number of places that year, and was viewed with suspicion by most landlords and landladies: a lone female interested in such a large flat, and without someone to share with immediately. I'd not expected that at all. So I told a lie. Mrs Ryan accepted that I'd eventually have some people sharing the place with me. She wasn't suspicious. That came later: when the flatmate didn't materialise.

'Anyone for that other room yet, Miss Wallace?'

I didn't mind her asking, but I did mind my lie. So I told her that I'd decided not to share the place after all.

'Well, you know now, Miss Wallace, I can't possibly allow you a reduction on the rent.'

That annoyed me.

I said: 'Did I say I wanted one, Mrs Ryan?'

'No, Miss Wallace, you didn't. I do apologise. It's just that it's such a big place for only one person ...' She was going to go on, but I interrupted her.

I said: 'I've lived in a bedsit for the past seventeen years.' That stopped her.

But I'm sure she eventually put two and two together. Perhaps.

I collected little in those seventeen years. You don't, when you live in one room. I moved from there to here with two black refuse sacks in a taxi. I'd left home in the same way, with the same number of bags. Funny! But I lived in both places – home and the bedsit – for the same length of time;

only a year in the difference. Leaving home was a much simpler act. More simple than leaving the bedsit. Leaving home was just that: leaving. There was no plan. No vision of the future. Nothing in the future to be thought about. What future do you think about at sixteen? Like a bird from the nest, I just left. But leaving the bedsit was different.

I was thirty-three. Everything is different at thirty-three. I'm sure no one will dispute that. Who among us does not have plans at that age? Plans underway. Plans laid. Plans abandoned. Plans backfiring. At thirty-three I had my plan, and because of that I was unsure. But certain, nonetheless. Odd, isn't it? At sixteen, I simply acted. Is that instinct, I wonder. I suppose it is. At sixteen I didn't say: 'I must leave this place in order to survive.'

I acted.

But leaving the bedsit was also an act of survival. Instinct again, I suppose. You can't beat it, can you?

Photographs. They were the only items other than my clothes which I took with me from that place. After stuffing my few, pathetic rags into the black bags, I went in search of those photos. It's not that I placed a lot of importance on them before that time, or since. So why did I take them? I had sufficient time to think about choosing a memento of home, and the house was empty at the time. It was easy for me to guess where they all were. My three sisters, all my junior, were dispersed between the neighbours after their day in school; it was a long-formed habit of theirs to avoid home and our father and the comfortless mothering I'd to offer: I was sixteen. Our father could have been in only one of two places – the pub or at work.

My mother was in her grave.

I don't take a final look around the place: I go in search of those photos.

'Final': perhaps at sixteen you don't think in such terms. 'Next' is the way you think at that age. So, next, after packing the bags, I took the photos. But it was final, it was the final act I performed in that house. Of course, I didn't know that back then.

They were in a drawer in a small table in the kitchen, the one on which the television stood. It was a grand table with beautifully turned legs. Mahogany, I now know. It was given to my mother by some old British couple she had once worked for. Boots and buckets piled beneath it, while its drawer held knots of rubbish and a cardboard chocolate box. The photos were in that box: a family of photos, smiles and togetherness and Sunday best; all the sacraments given to a family recorded, marriage, christenings, communions, confirmation, all black and white. The box was packed, photos forcing at the lid, which was securely held in place by a tight elastic band. And Christmas cards, used ones. You know, ones held over from the previous Christmas: 'To make the place look cheerful,' she would say.

She was friendless.

I took four photos. One of me on my mother's knee, bald, a baby; another of my sisters and myself, the school photo. There's no date on it. I don't remember the event. I also took my first communion photo. And one of my mother. A beautiful studio photograph of her. She's half sitting against a low table. Her hair is wavy, to her shoulders. She's wearing a short-sleeved, dark-coloured dress, and high-heels. It's in black and white. I know nothing about this photo, when, where, why. Taken before marriage, because her hair in the wedding photo, which is also the one used in her mortuary card, is short. That photo in the mortuary card: a badly focused shot of a grinning woman with a white skull-cap type of hat perched on the side of her head, from which a feather sticks out. White: virginity? or surrender? I wonder.

I always feel there's something ironic about those wedding photos on mortuary cards. I can understand that for many, at that time, their wedding photo was probably the only photo taken of them as adults. But that wasn't the case with my mother.

Interesting that I should choose photos of my mother as woman, mother, but not wife.

Seventeen years in a bedsit.

Sounds pathological. Some would say I lived alone for too long. As though my life began when I was sixteen. Your life begins once, and only once. I'm sure there are those who think I must have been naked and new at that tender age. Innocent. Well, I wasn't innocent, but I was ignorant: memory had yet to find its course to knowledge. Memory is a funny matter. I guess it all depends on the particular type of memory.

Once, when I was small, I'd a plaster on the hairy part of my arm. When it was time to remove it, I spent nearly the entire day peeling it off, bit by bit, bit by bit, inflicting manageable amounts of pain on myself.

Memory is like that; the process of rebuilding the facts.

Anyway, when I'd the plaster carefully removed, I began examining the wound. At first, simply looking, gradually succumbing to the perverse childish desire to touch it, just to see if it still hurt. We've all done that, haven't we? And if it did still hurt, we'd leave it alone, eventually forgetting about it. Then, one day, we'd notice the scar. Pain then a memory. The wound then different. Flesh never again to be the same.

A scar becomes a sterile place. Hair doesn't grow there any more. It remains a reminder.

So, at sixteen, you could say I'd yet to ... remember, I suppose. There's nothing unusual in that. The 'present' is the only 'time' to any teenager, with the future being their focus. That focus changes as we grow older because the future suddenly holds death. At that stage, the future is too close so the focus becomes the past: happiness, or even anger and resentment are more easy to live with than dread.

Out. Away. That's what I wanted at sixteen. First, I got a job.

9

Krups. Weighing scales and food-mixers. 'Come to work in Krups.' That's what the sticker said on the window of the bus. That was the early 1970s for you. But that's not all! I went up to the factory, no application form, no nothing; asked the receptionist about getting a job. She told me to take a seat, which I did. Within a short time a man came to talk with me. A Mr Draper. I remember him well. Friendly. His eyes were his face, brown, large, slow to blink, moist and dreamy, like a camel's. Must have been in his thirties, then.

He knew. He put two and two together, quickly.

'Where do you live?'

I tell him.

'Yes, I know the place well. My wife and I often go there to the lake. They've done wonders with it over the years.' He pauses, thinking deeply, like one recalling the name of an old acquaintance. 'Wasn't there some sort of tragedy out there a few years back?'

'Yes.'

'A fire. Some woman died, I believe.'

'Yes.'

'You knew her?'

'Yes.'

'Tell me all about yourself.'

I tell.

'You left school at fourteen. Why?'

I tell him the reason: the death of my mother.

'I see. When was that?'

I tell him.

'I see,' he says, slowly. There is hesitation. I can see other questions hovering in his face, in his eyes. He was putting two and two together, I suppose.

I can see now that his next question was well thought out.

'Your mother was ill for long?'

'No,' I say.

He blinks. He asks, after a moment, if I can start on the

following Monday.

And that is how I got my job.

For the first month or so I cycled there each day on my mother's High Lizzy. I hated that bike. I used to leave it pedal-propped against the kerb near the entrance gate, out of sight, unlocked, hoping it would be stolen. It wasn't. When my father knew that I'd a job, he threatened to throw me out. I said nothing. Then, one Thursday I got a half-day off work, bought the *Limerick Leader*, picked a couple of bedsits from it. Phoned. Made an appointment to see one. Took it. Got a taxi home that evening. Moved out.

Moved in.

The bike remained in its usual place for quite some time. Months later, when I went to see if it was still there, I was neither happy nor sad to see that it had disappeared.

Living there for seventeen years was much like having lived at home for sixteen. Both lives can be, more or less, broken up into five-year periods. The first five years of childhood and the first five years in the bedsit were similar, I suppose. I knew nothing of the world. Like a child, I was learning from the actions and behaviour of others: getting my fingers burned. And everything was fun. I was, for a while, new.

The first item I bought for the bedsit was an alarm clock. Then some dishcloths and towels. Necessary things. There were blankets, but no sheets. I didn't buy sheets or pillow covers. And a radio – I bought a radio. A clothes iron. As I said, I bought only necessary things.

Routine: either good or bad, like a mossless rolling stone. It deadens those with spirit, yet others will thrive, their lives decided for them. I chose, I sought routine because I had to survive. The nothing I had needed to seem important.

On Wednesday I'd arrive back from work at a quarter to five, like any other week-day. I'd have something to eat.

Toast and a boiled egg maybe. Then I'd wash my hair, and in the same water I'd wash my clothes, knickers and stuff like that; the stuff I used to feel embarrassed about at the launderette.

I always felt slightly uneasy on Wednesday evenings. Just slightly. Sometimes I'd decide to clean the cooker or something. Maybe do some ironing. I didn't have a television. That seemed like too big a decision, then. If it was summer, I'd go to the park, walk around the trees, maybe sit on the grass if there weren't too many people. Other times I'd walk down by the Shannon. If 'poor man's Kilkee' was empty, I'd sit there on one of the stone benches, admiring the rushing water. More often than not, I just sat at my window, watching the street. My room was on the second floor, so I'd a good view of that street. There was a take-away directly across the way, along with other shops, a chemist, butcher and such-like. And a taxi rank, also. I would sometimes sit for hours on end at that window. In darkness. Well, not darkness as such, but that permanent half-gloom of a town at night. What I mean by darkness is that I'd not have turned on the light in my room.

I savour stillness yet. Calmness.

I loved to watch people, a novelty for someone from the country, where there are few people in a person's day. I loved to catch them scratching their arses or picking their noses or admiring their reflections in shop windows, even talking to themselves. Couples having restrained arguments, or otherwise. I loved especially to observe the customers at the take-away. Some would already be opening their white bundle as they left the hatch, hungrily sucking in chips that were obviously too hot. Others would leave with their white bundles intact, as though indifferent to the upcoming feast. Cars pulled up there, and I'd be witness to the debate that went on as the occupants decided on their meal. If it was a family, then the mother did the buying while the father stayed with the kids, eyeing all the young ones that passed by. And if it was a young couple out for the night, then it was he who did the buying while she sat in the car preening herself in the rear view mirror, examining those in her own age group who passed by. I really loved to watch people watching others.

The scene in the street seldom varied on those summer Wednesday evenings. Gradually the street lights would come on earlier and earlier. The people there would darken; their summer shades shed.

Winter. I would still go out for a walk on winter Wednesday evenings; sometimes to the park, even though it was closed at six o'clock. But that didn't matter, not to me. I could still walk beneath the trees which overhung the railings. I got into the habit of preparing a stew for myself during that first winter. It passed the time, on Wednesday: all that chopping. And while it cooked, I sat in my unlit room, watching the world outside.

Thursday was pay day, and pay day was cause for a minor celebration that evening. A few drinks – that's all. The *Limerick Leader* came out on Thursday. We'd have it with us that evening in the pub, checking to see who was playing where: bands in dancehalls. We? Well, I suppose it would be more correct to say 'they'.

They. They were the group I became a part of in Krups. It would have been difficult not to belong to a group of one kind or another. The majority of the workforce is female; teenagers and twenty-year-olds, coming mostly from the nearby housing estates. They overwhelmed me. All of them, not just the group I knew. They all seemed so familiar with each other. They reminded me of creatures in a litter. Happy. Loving. Close. Secure. They shared everything: troubles, sanitary towels, money, clothes, tears, troubles.

They fascinated me. I amused them.

It was my quietness, I suppose. They took me to themselves as one takes a stray dog. They straightened me out. Subtly. I had head-lice. Yes. No surprise, really. The

13

preening and prettying of adolescence is not for all. Like childhood, as I said earlier. Childhood is no guarantee of innocence. So when they handed me a vinegar bottle with a small amount of clear, pungent liquid, for my itchy dandruff, I knew what they were doing. I knew they viewed me as someone who was innocent. They may even have thought I was a fool. But how could I say I knew more about life than lice? The order of things had been altered, leaving me without language, like a child, when a child.

If Thursday was celebration day, then Friday saw the final preparations getting underway.

We'd an hour for lunch, and during that time some would wash their hair, getting a friend to blow-dry it for them; eyebrows were plucked, again by a friend. They offered to trim the dead-ends from my hair – after my dandruff was gone. Plucked my eyebrows, too, they did. They shared out creams and ointments for spots and pimples. Cleansers and creams of all sorts passed from one to the other. One day, a girl called Rita took an anti-perspirant aerosol from her bag of tricks, shook it, grimaced. She said: 'It's nearly empty; better get another. Here, you have it.' I took it. Emery boards flashed. Nails were varnished. Make-up for the face and eyes was discussed – endlessly. And the Avon catalogue was scrutinised. Rita was the one to order the vaginal spray – for the laugh. They laughed. I was learning.

And then there was the singing. It usually started after three o'clock on Friday, lasting for an hour or so. Pop songs mostly. *Bobby's Girl* was one. *Streets of London* was another. All together and all alone they would sing, each lost in her own world, faces somewhat sad, like a person in prayer or singing a hymn. There was a dance-like quality to their working bodies as they sang. I'd watch the back of the girl before me, her hunched navy-clad shoulders dodging this way and that, like a boxer, a perfect rhythm to her movements as she screwed nameless bits into the guts of the product, the pneumatic screwdivers dangling in front of her from bright-yellow coils. Our left arms would shoot out simultaneously, like that of some helpless spastic, ready to place our respective pieces and scoop the next lot from the line as it soldiered on and on and on, all in thirty-six point four-two seconds flat.

'Come on Elizabeth, join in, can't you,' the girl from across the line roars. *Bobby's Girl* is the song being sung and she is making big eyes and a bigger mouth as she substitutes Bobby for Tom, her latest. I smile.

So, on Friday we parted, not with goodbyes, but with the reaffirming of times and places:

'Half-seven, at the Brazen Head.'

'I'll be at the stage by half-nine. Wait there for me, will you?'

'We'll call to your place at eight – be ready now, mind.'

On Friday night I had fun.

Next day I would awaken at noon, or thereabouts. I'd have a hangover; head still buzzing with the sound of loud music, chest tight from all that I'd smoked, stomach laden with fish and chips. But there was no time to think: there was the autopsy to be performed on the previous night. Usually we met in a pub. No alcohol. Soda-water and lime or cups of coffee and talk, talk, talk:

'Did you see this one? Did you see that one? What d'you think of yer man with the black hair, blond hair, brown hair, red hair, fair hair, straight, curly or short or long? Did you see him looking at me? Was he looking for long? What way did he look? Would you say he fancies me? Was he up dancing with anyone else? Bitch! Will he be there next week, d'you think? Will he ask me up then, d'you think? What'll I wear, do you think? Will she be there, d'you think? Bitch! You should've seen the way he was lampin' you. You should've seen the way he was lampin' yer one. Bitch! Why didn't he make a date, d'you think?'

Partings again were the emphasising of times and places.

There's one girl in particular whom I should mention. She was not part of my group. She worked on the production line across from me. Frances Cleary. Frankie, she preferred to be called. A tomboy. Boyish haircut. Jeans, jumpers worn loose, and brogues. Her face wasn't pretty. Attractive, yes. Interesting, to me. She always seemed so jolly. So full of life. Smiling, always. She giggled. It was an infectious sound. And I knew it was hers as it gurgled above the noise of the machinery. I would smile, as a mother does to the pleasure-purr from a child. She never wore an overall, although the majority did, including myself. Even those others who didn't wear an overall looked so conscious of their bodies as they walked about the factory, their arms folded beneath their breasts, hiding or de-emphasising them, bowing their heads or turning their faces as they passed a group of men.

Of course there were those who flaunted themselves. Tight tops. Tight jeans. Short skirts. But they were different. They were beyond my cognisance. I was afraid of them. I was embarrassed by them. I would have been dumb in their presence. Frankie Cleary was someone I could wish to be. Envious is how I felt on seeing the pert swing of her boyish body as she sauntered through the aisles. I noticed her lips. Moist lips. Lips of a person who smiles a lot, like the moist nose of a happy dog. Watching her was an escape. To me, she was sexless; a happy human. Sexless, as I say.

She noticed me watching her. It amused her, I now know. She winked at me one day. I blushed. She laughed, getting the girls who worked beside her to look at me. They laughed too.

I stopped watching.

I would hurry back to the bedsit on Saturday afternoon, dump my dirty clothes in a refuse sack, and hurry to the launderette. It was usually empty by then. The first time I went there it was during the morning. Packed with women. Mothers, commanding mountains of multi-coloured clothes.

Bundling them in disgust into the washers. Folding and smoothing and caressing them when taking them from the drier. They chatted and laughed while they waited, oblivious to others who weren't mothers. It was as if they looked upon the amount you had for washing as an indication of your status. Their voices dipped to a whisper when discussing their intimate problems; guffawing out loud at something which amused them. I decided to go there instead in the evening. It was mostly people like myself, then. Single people. Silent people. Devoid of pride in washed clothes. Embarrassed youths: college types, swotting while waiting. Girls my age, reading magazines and eyeing the college types, being ignored by the college types. I would sit there. Still. Watching. I'd get myself a fish and chip on the way back to the bedsit, looking onto the Saturday evening street as I ate. Then I'd sleep for a while. Later I would wash my hair; preparations for another night of fun.

Sunday. I would stay in bed until three or four. I'd wake up at maybe twelve or one, but sleep on. It felt good to rest. Sometimes I'd cook myself a dinner – fried chop, mashed potato, tinned peas. Usually I'd have to go out to get the meat, a mean, tired-looking chop – dear and dangerous, sold in one of those small supermarket-type shops, family-run, selling everything from bootlaces to hair combs and as much dust as you could hope for. But if the day wasn't nice, or if I didn't feel like getting dressed to go out, I'd make some mash and have a packet of soup with it. Maybe I'd fry myself an egg or two or three.

On Sunday I would take a shower, my only shower of the week. The shower and toilet were on the floor above me. I'd bought myself – my first – dressing gown and slippers so as to avoid having to get dressed immediately after showering. I hated forcing my hot, showered body into air-less jeans and tops, but it took me a long time before I could bring myself to wear that dressing gown. I always felt so naked, and would have died if I'd met anyone on my way

17

back from the bathroom, which was always likely. I remember once actually standing at my door, dressing gown on over knickers and bra, soap in one hand, towel in the other, ten pence for the meter clutched in my fist, heart beating. No. I couldn't do it. The pay phone on the floor below rang, and that did it.

Sunday and Dromkeen was like Sunday and mass. It was Mecca. I knew of it before coming to live in Limerick. A bus used to stop at the top of our dead-end road every Sunday night, full already of smiling faces. Into it would file the smiling faces from that dead-end road, joined by other smiling faces from the surrounding area. I could smell their smell when they were gone: perfume and cigarettes and fun. I'd have been watching them before the arrival of that red, lumbering bus. Hidden and sad and dirty and happy and angry, I would watch.

'What are you so down in the mouth for?' one of them asked on my first trip there. We were speeding along on the bus from Limerick, happy faces all around, the smell of perfume and cigarettes and fun. It was like visiting Santa Claus, for me, half joy, half something else.

Dromkeen dance-hall was in the middle of nowhere. The building still stands, but without its dancers. I've been told that second-hand furniture is sold there now, the dance floor crowded with cookers and couches and beds and chairs, the used and abused stuff of homes piled on the spot where the stuff of homes once started. I can imagine young couples waltzing through all that stuff, hoping for that bargain. It's at a crossroad, on the main Tipperary-Limerick road. Buses of all descriptions and from all directions with people of all descriptions and from all directions, converged on Dromkeen of a Sunday night and the occasional Friday night. All types came. It was a time when Ireland was becoming young. I can see that now. It was evident in Dromkeen.

Left-overs from the time when every dance was either a

waltz or a jive were there: men displaying respectability in the respectable darkness of the Sunday suit, striped tie, pioneer pin, black patent slip-on shoes, Brylcreem. The woman he wanted sat by the cloakroom wall: immaculate, stiff, black skirt, stout ankle, blouse with bow, black patent high-heels with exposed toe, Mary-medal at neck or fixed to watch strap.

Sunday Suit parades past, eyeing Exposed Toe, who ignores Sunday Suit until a look can be taken without Exposed Toe compromising herself. Beyond all that, on the dance floor, are the younger men and women: jeans, sweat-shirts, cheese-cloth shirts. Long-haired young men stand and watch groups of young women enjoying themselves, dancing, swaying, rhythmically slouching about, handbags piled in a heap, around which they circle. Boyfriend and girlfriend couples dance beside them, matching cheese-cloth shirts and bell-bottom jeans, with either clogs or desert boots, and long hair, and star-sign pendants, and wrist-watches threaded through wide strips of studded leather. Four-Seven-Eleven battling with patchouli, battling with Old Spice, battling with patchouli, feet, underarms, alcohol, cigarettes, pot, piss. Pioneer Pin and Exposed Toe take to the floor to waltz stiffly, swiftly and in silence, moving to the comfort of something like *The Ring Your Mother Wore,* swing-ing past island columns of almost stationary unisex-dressed couples kneading each other, probing tongue with tongue, bodies nudging; ignored by shocked Exposed Toe, though not entirely ignored by Pioneer Pin. The tempo then changes; the band remembering their contract to play something for everyone: keep all patrons dancing. Some-times it all became too much for Pioneer Pin; he'd be eyeing all those loose-looking young ones: drooling, hands stuffed in his pockets: itching his itch. He gets one up on the floor for the fast set: his mind on the possibility of the slow. And she accepts – just for the laugh: this is going to be fun. Around him she gyrates, eyes closed in mock seriousness; he apes around after her, embarrassed, driven, ludicrous-looking, the music now pounding out.

'God, there's great energy in you all the same,' he roars at her over the noise.

'You're not doing too bad yourself,' she replies, throwing a glance to the sideline to see the effect on her laughing friends, beyond whom is Exposed Toe, watching: marking the man. Disgusted.

'There's a right little bitch, if I ever saw one.' Her friends nod, lips tight.

But we meant no harm, no harm at all. It was only a bit of fun.

Then there was 'outside'; a mixture of boast and scandal:

'She went "outside" at twelve o'clock ... We went "outside", well, it must have been half-eleven, or thereabouts.'

'Outside.' Kissing. Practising. Intercourse. Practising. 'Outside' was a feature of Dromkeen because so many travelled there by bus.

'D'you want to go "outside"?' – usually for air, was the equivalent to the townies' 'Can I walk you home?' Both amounted to the same thing really. 'Outside' usually meant being pinned against the wall by a horny young fellah, French kissing, kneading a breast with one hand, groping in your crotch with the other, interrupting these operations in order to keep your hand on his crotch; sometimes he might – simultaneously – be holding a discussion with you, like: 'Do you come here often', or, 'Where do you live?' It was innocent stuff: unless he actually took it out.

'I have to,' he'd say, starting to masturbate, leaning with one hand against the wall, where you left him: his lost prop. Looking back, you'd see him working himself: Fast. Faster. Pulling. Pulling. Pulling. Squeeze. Pull. Squeeze. Pull. Squeeze. Pull. Pull. Faster. Squeezing. Squeezing. Pull. Faster. Squeeze. Faster. Faster. Faster. Faster. Uh!

If intercourse was the objective, then the bus was the

place: 'Your bus or mine?' And if a fellah had a car, well ... he had a hotel.

There were some who kissed a little and talked a lot, strolling, smoking, standing a little apart. Nice.

Monday. Swollen lips. Tits, too. Broke. Necks bitten. Tits, too. Tales swapped of things done:

'He put it in, but didn't come'

'I let him, with a johnny.'

'I let him, in my knickers.'

'I let him, it was safe.'

'I let him, twice, once from behind.'

'I let him, in my mouth.'

'I let him, standing by the wall.'

'I let him, in the back seat of the car.'

'I let him, in the front seat of the car.'

'I let him, in the bus.'

'I let him, from behind, standing against the car, resting my arms on the wing.'

'I let him, sitting across him in the car ... in the bus.'

'I let him, on the grass.'

'I let him, and his friend.'

'I let him, up my arse.'

These tales passed between twos, initially. Confessionally. Then passed between twos again. Sensationally. Such chat was a feature of Monday. Fact? Fiction? Fantasy? It was hard to tell ... though sometimes ...

Subdued. That's the type of day Monday was. Everybody tired. And real. Devoid of finery and expectation. Sleep on the mind. Mine too. That evening I'd have a fish and chip, in bed. A pot of tea, milked and sugared, beside me on the floor. And sleeping before the time for sleep, I'd drift off to the sound of a world outside my window, above me, outside my door.

Tuesday. The day I shopped for food and tidied and cooked something to eat. Refreshed. Then Wednesday; a week passed, a month, a year, time.

Seasons came and went. The seasons' extremes – summer and winter – were times of extremes for me, then. Summers in the sun. Eight-berth caravans in places like Ballybunion and Tramore. Two whole weeks of fun. Two whole weeks of not sleeping alone. Two whole weeks of being a part of that tension once again: the tension of not being alone. I didn't understand that. Not then. I mean, when someone says to you: 'Jesus! Elizabeth, you can't stay alone in that bedsit for two whole weeks: you'll go mad,' – well, you accept that. It makes sense. It is the right thing to go and be with others. Like a child going to Santa Claus. A thing done. Always. So, I went.

It was the night-time that bothered me most. Not exactly night, but the early morning, when the effects of the alcohol had worn off.

Someone's breathing, or snoring, or movement disturbs me. Eyes open on an unfamiliar world: roof too close, window too small, in the wrong place, curtains with the wrong pattern, too hot, bed too small, too hard, who's that? I see sleeping shapes, humps of blankets, heads of hair. Who is that? Philomena? Mary? Amanda? Mother? No. Not home.

I'd slept with Philomena, my sister. That changed after Mary came, then I slept with my mother. He slept in a room of his own, a room in which I sometimes slept. After the funeral, he moved into the bed of his dead wife.

I leave my bed on those holiday mornings by the sea. Their beds I carefully pass. Faces on pillows. Deadly. Rigid. True. Rigid and true like masks. Slackened smiles revealing something else. Revealing another. I wake up there feeling awkward. Just awkward. Nothing more. Silently I leave the caravan. Down to the shore I go, walking, listening to the sea.

We spent our days in many ways. Prowling the streets, loud: to be seen; on the beach, loud: to be seen; in the shops, loud: to be seen; the evening dangling before us. The caravan then a beauty parlour. Heads turbaned in towels, faces creamed, nails shiny with wet coats of varnish, a cassette player winding out the latest chart toppers, choruses bellowed out by all, ointments and lotions applied to sunburnt shoulders, pimples bruised, blackheads steamed, Rita lying on the floor, hauling up the zip of her air-tight jeans with a shoelace, arses in jeans analysed from every angle, breasts too, cigarette butts in cups, swelling in the dredges of coffee or tea, tissue paper everywhere, smeared with cream and lipstick and varnish and ear-wax and make-up, clothes abandoned in a multi-coloured pile, smell of perfume, smell of anti-perspirant, smell of toothpaste: smell of purpose.

I occasionally allowed them to 'do' my face, just for the fun of it, removing it immediately, though. It was like being called Betty, seeing myself like that. They'd get me to tuck my shirt inside my jeans: 'Give 'em a hint of the promised land, Elizabeth.'

The night ahead was as you'd expect: fun, frolics – frenetic.

Back to the caravan we'd stagger, arms linked, singing, laughing. Others in the caravan park roared out at us to be quiet, causing us to stiffen momentarily, double up and separate, isolating ourselves from the infectiousness of each other's choking laughter. It was I who usually had the key. The dependable one: hallmark of the uncherished. You know the type: call them and they come running, delighted in not being unacknowledged, confusing abuse with love. Like the delight of the work-weary child at the praise it receives for performing those unpleasant tasks: 'Who's the best around here at washing dishes? – for bringing in the coal? – for minding the baby? – for? – well, who's Daddy's little girl?' So, even at seventeen you still feel delight in that sort of acknowledgement. You become the minder of keys, the lender of money, the runner of errands, the phoner for taxis. Once, at work, they made a collection to buy a present for someone who'd just had a baby. It was I who took the morning off in order to buy this present. I didn't know her. I was chosen to do this: I was chosen to belong. I felt so less lost. For a while only.

They argued with each other, in the morning, in the caravan by the sea. I hated it. It surprised me, their bickering. It didn't make sense. They always seemed so close. Sometimes it started while I was there, other times they'd've started while I was out on my morning walk. It could be something quite simple like, who was going to make the tea, or whose turn it was to tidy up the kitchen. Initially, I moved to do the task: reflex reaction. Keeper of the peace: hallmark of the uncertain, of the uncherished. You know the type: always battling with a guilty blush, even though they've nothing to hide. They always feel – acutely – that they've done something wrong, they're to blame, it's all their fault, everything would be different if only they were better, different, smarter, quieter, quicker, prettier, dead. Some snap. Some don't. I did. In childhood. An instinctive reaction. Untempered. Guilt, then. Guilt, always. But also something else, like, say, a satisfaction.

She says: 'How did this get in my boot?' holding on high, delicately like a host, a razorblade, the red of her blood on her thumb. Her toe, the big one on her left foot, bleeds. She continues to explain how she felt something pinching her toe. I hear it all on another level. Our eyes are locked. Both wondering. Both disbelieving. She not believing that I, her daughter, could have done such a thing. Why? And I not believing that she *must* suspect something. As she says: who could have done such a thing? I am calm. She, bewildered.

'Who could have done this?' her eyes searching mine.

'I don't know.' There is silence. Nothing at all but a

hissing in my ears.

'Will I get you a basin of water?' I don't hear my own voice.

'For what?'

'For your toe.'

'My toe?'

'Yes. Your toe.'

'Yes, my toe. Do.'

I did. There is relief in action.

I was ten.

She says: 'Who did this?' Words from her as she points to the red streak on a white floor-tile in the kitchen. A stain left by a felt marker. It is not I. I do not have a red marker. But I redden when my eyes meet hers: the old guilt dawning.

'It'll come off with paraffin.'

'It better.'

So. Even at seventeen you still submit to that old guilt, regardless: force of habit, or force of conscience? It's all the one, really.

Tense. That's how I felt when they bickered; a familiar feeling: a family feeling.

Christmas. Another extreme. A jolly time. The Krups Social. The dinner dance. Rows of intimidating tables. Blocks of white, patterned with an intimidating array of knives, forks and spoons flank the polished square of the dance floor. Familiar men looking strange in tie, shirt and suit. Women and girls in long dresses. Bodies revealed: breasts, waists and arses. The unattached males grouped together at the bar, doing double-take stares: intimidated by us, the unattached females. We are ladies, restricted into refinement by the clothes we wear. We troop in groups to the loo, arms folded: nonchalant. My arse! We are conscious of every move we make.

Those who have boyfriends sit in triumphant isolation, silent. Those who are married arrive in foursome groups, chatting women followed by bored-looking husbands: not looking as triumphant in their isolation. And that's how the tables fill: married groups, couples and the unattached, all finding their own club.

Let the night begin!

Outfits analysed. Outfits criticised. Figures envied. Figures pitied. Husbands scrutinised. Wives scrutinised. Whisper. Whisper. Whisper. 'What did he ever see in her? What did she ever see in him?' Self-consciously we spoon up our canned fruit cocktail, never batting an eyelid, but wondering nonetheless – dessert *before* dinner? Lips smack, smack, smack: 'Um! That was lovely.' Pulling at our mouths with our paper napkins. Glad that that part is over. Plates of turkey and ham follow bowls of salty mushroom soup. Sweaty waitresses, black skirt, white blouse – cheap labour – splonk domes of mash, watery carrots and hard Brussels sprouts beside the tongues of meat. We eat. Fastidiously. Self-consciously. Furtively eyeing each other. Lips smack, smack, smack: 'Um! That was lovely. Meat was tender. Mash was lovely. Stuffing was delicious.' Then apple tart and cream or sherry trifle. 'Tea or coffee?'

It is the bright-red colour of carrot you recognise on puking the whole lot up before the night is over.

After the meal, the speech. The manager thanking us for something and looking forward to more of it during the coming year. His wife, we were told by the old crowd, wore the same dress every year. A plain black number. Disconcerting. Galling even.

Then the spot-prizes: 'First man up to the stage with a pair of women's tights wins a ...' It was so funny. And finally the band: 'All right, ladies and gentlemen, time now for ye to work off some of that dinner ye've been stuffing yerselves with all night. Let's see ye all up now enjoying yerselves.' Cue for a rush to the dance floor, bar and loo.

Photographers swoop upon the foursomes. Pictures in the following week's *Leader*: At the annual Krups' dinner dance in Cruise's Hotel were, from left – two smiling pairs.

We had a camera of our own: 'Here's so-and-so with so-and-so and so-and-so', either eating the dinner or standing by a wall. You'd see a sober group photo.

'Here's so-and-so and so-and-so up dancing.' You'd see a couple in profile and the flash-startled faces of other dancers.

'Here's one of so-and-so drinking a pint. It was so funny.' You'd see so-and-so's mouth wide open, eyes bulb-bright, a stranger looking on.

'Here's so-and-so kissing so-and-so.' You'd see the tops of their heads and the upside down bottles hanging behind the bar.

'It was so funny. Here's so-and-so sitting on the loo.' You'd see so-and-so with her head hidden in her lap, helplessly embarrassed, knickers about her knees, and the back of the person who had forced open the toilet door. You'd see photos of the tops of heads, sides of faces, close-ups gone horribly wrong; bits of ceiling, bits of floor, bits of bodies – it was just so funny.

It passed like that, Christmas did.

It passed like that, a year did, and another, and another, four, five. Time.

By the time I was twenty-one they were gone, that group. Marriage mostly. Pushing babies in H.P. buggies. Shot-gun marriages mostly. Morning sickness coinciding with the engagement ring. Bulky brides in virgin white. Pimply, po-faced youths with manly moustaches. Faces grave like on communion and confirmation day. Marriage: last sacrament bar one. So they went. Some worked until the baby came, availed of maternity leave and then left for good. Those who continued working gradually drifted into groups of other mothers; grannies, older married sisters or out of work husbands minding the babies. Flats they lived in, or with in-laws, or in caravans beside cottages in the country, staying there until they had sufficient babies to graduate to a house in South Hill or Moyross: those sufficient babies becoming the 'joy-riding' crop.

Around me they changed like leaves on trees.

The first to leave from that group was Rita – a city girl, slim, blonde and very beautiful. She had beauty without haughtiness, which left her stranded. The older women on the production line regarded her with pity, while the younger ones saw her as a rival with an unfair advantage.

'Hide your man! Rita's coming.'

It was a joke, and it wasn't.

While the rest of us, average in every respect, attracted the attentions of the apprentice fitters and electricians who worked in the factory, Rita attracted the older men, the qualified men, the married men, the men who knew all about it. This only amused her. We were impressed, intimidated further.

'Go-on-there-you-boyo!'

That's what the older men would growl-grunt at any young apprentice caught chatting to Rita. She would smile and the boy would leave, red-faced.

I was closer to her than any of the others, for she had a way of being all things to all people, a chameleon, protecting herself. She was the only one ever to come to my bedsit. She was the only one I ever invited. I knew the others wondered at our friendship, wondered what could we possibly have in common. I liked her. She amused me. She was always fun – always had a quick word, sexual innuendo slipping easily and with mock-shame from her tongue. It was she who bought the vaginal spray from the Avon catalogue: 'Air freshener,' she grimaced, shooting a shot up her skirt, 'in case strangers call.' I laughed at first from shock, learning slowly to laugh for fun. She gave me that.

28

'He's a yoke between his legs like a bicycle pump: the filthy bastard,' she gushes in my ear, breathless, after abandoning on the dance-floor the boy with whom she's been slow dancing. 'God forgive me and it Sunday night an' all,' blessing herself, her eyes wandering after him.

'Let him find someone with a tube that needs filling,' my reply to her, but a copy, a poor variation of her many quick quips. We bend heads together, doubling over in laughter.

We swapped tales in the street-lit gloom of my bedsit; tales of tired mothers beaten by drunken fathers. Of shame. Of rage. It was healing, like confession – as though the guilt was ours – to speak in the dark to each other.

'I hate him,' we said, from the thinking silence, from the thinking depths yet to be fathomed. She was a shock, like an echo, eerie at first. And like an echo, true, compulsive, wanting to say more to hear more to say more. I listened. I responded. We made pacts while tearful or drunk: we'll not live the lives of our mothers. This knowledge of each other became our bond.

She asked me one night about my mother. I refrained from delivering the usual lie of death-due-to-illness. It was a shock. It was turmoil. I was agitated. Can I? Will I? Tears welled.

'You don't have to, if you don't want to,' she said.

'I do. I do. I do.' I felt fearful of her rejection. I started rummaging through the bedsit, mumbling about showing a photograph of my mother.

'I must show you this photo of her first.' I kept saying this as I pulled out drawers and cleared the wardrobe. I was sobbing, but it felt like laughter. 'It's here, somewhere, I know it is. It has to be.' But nothing. I started to panic, to feel angry. 'Where is the fucking thing?' I sobbed, throwing clothes everywhere. Pulling. Dragging. Frantic. I tripped, my foot caught in the tangle of a jumper's sleeve. I fell backwards, landing on the mat of clothes, my head just barely missing the wall. I saw it all: the wardrobe to my left, bed straight ahead by the other wall, door to my right, worktop and sink beside it, ceiling beyond the light, darkness beyond the top of the window: I opened my mouth.

She told me about the scream. I knew about the tears.

'Whenever you're ready,' she said.

'Yes,' I promised.

She became quieter around that time. Less talkative. Less fun. Because of me, I thought. I became anxious. Some time had passed since that night of the photo.

I watched for her arrival one evening; she was staying with me for the weekend. I was at my usual position, by the window, with the room in darkness. I saw her coming. I moved. Deliberately. Kneeling by my bed, I hauled from beneath it the box containing those photos. A white shoebox. I left it on the bed. Conspicuous. Like the white coffin of a dead infant. I made tea. We made small talk. We were both anxious. She sat on the bed, tea in hand. I sat beside her, the box behind us.

'I ...' We started together, then laughed nervously.

'Go on,' I said to her.

'My periods are ten days overdue.'

She let him ... she was curious ... he'd pulled it out ... there was a mess on her stomach ... but you never know ... it only takes a bit to do the trick ... she could have stopped him ... but he promised ... he'd it out ... hard and hot ... oh! God ... his fingers ... down there ... slapping into her ... she could've burst ... she came ... God, it was awful ... she was dizzy ... had to lie down ... got on top of her ... please! please! please! ... no! no! no! ... it was hot and throbbing and ready to burst ... he slipped it in, the bastard, then took it out, the bastard ... bit the fucker in the ear ... thought he'd stop ... rubbed it there ... rocking like a dog ... tongue in my mouth ... in a bit ... just a little bit ... another bit ... up to the hilt ... doing the clappers ... had it out in time, he said.

She should have had them on the Wednesday of the previous week.

She'd a pimple on her neck ... that was a good sign ... she was craving for chocolate ... another good sign ... but no sign at all of them, yet ... what would she do? ... she couldn't have ... she couldn't marry him ... not him! ... he didn't make a date for the weekend ... did I think she was? ... would I say he pulled out in time? ... would I say she looked different? ... would I say she'd get them after this length of time? ... did I think she could get caught so close to her periods? ... they say if you drink neat gin while sitting in a hot bath ... or bump on your arse down a flight of stairs ... Oh! Jesus, Mary and Joseph, what am I going to do!

Her periods came that evening. She burst into the room after coming back from the loo, a smear of blood on the long finger of her right hand, blessing herself, laughing, triumphant, a spot of blood on her forehead.

One year later she was married to another guy; three months pregnant going down the aisle. I was not at the wedding. Our bond had been broken: her anger was a lie. How else could she have done what she did? She would live the life of her mother. A life of babies and beatings. The stupid fucking bitch, I thought as she talked on that night.

I'd replaced the white shoebox beneath the bed before she came back from the loo.

She, like the rest, became tatty and dull when married. Sang the glory of weather that dried clothes, marvelled at meat, cheap and tender, spoke of bargains and thrift. Nights spent by the TV, bloated from new foods: novelties in bright boxes, to be baked, grilled or fried; fattening, gradually, him and her. You'd meet them at a disco once or twice before the baby came, he avoiding old friends, embarrassed by his big-bellied wife; she, on her lap of honour, indifferent to the indifference, his hand gripped tightly. She, like the rest, was all backache, bladder and breasts, cutting in with a groan as we shared our night's exploits. She, like many, didn't return to work after the baby. She, like those, was envied, then forgotten.

We dragged her out to the hen party of the next to take flight. She came, wearing Scholl sandals on her feet, her skirt down at the front and up at the back, her body neither lean nor fleshy, just simply no longer tailored to attract.

'Married life,' she declared, poking me in the ribs with her left elbow, halfway through that night. Before me was her hand, fingers spread like spokes. Bleary-eyed, I focused on the rings ranged as far as the knuckle on her ring finger, gold, diamonds and rubies. I smiled, remembering the multi-coiled rings used for identifying hens. The hand turned over, fingertips bowing to the palm, a fist displaying four naked nails.

'Hm?' she huffed, questioning my response to their condition – colourless and cracked.

We were both nineteen.

The breaking up of that group was as imperceptible as it was definite, like autumn trees accepting their winter nakedness. One Thursday evening I arrived at the usual place, a packed place, but empty of the people I knew, had known. I went straight to the cloakroom, urged to do so by the agitation I experienced there and then. 'Mary Loves John.' A statement encased in a lipstick heart on the toilet door where I pissed. I then walked to Perry Square, pacing beneath the bare trees.

There was a clothes-line in the bathroom. A plastic-coated wire stretching over the bath. I only ever used it to hang up my clothes while taking a shower. Sometimes I'd see a man's shirt there, usually white, dripping rapidly and smelling of washing powder, then stiff-dry, displaying stains. But mostly the line remained unused, gathering a skin of dust. So it was a surprise for me to see several pairs of tights arrayed there one evening. Obviously someone new had come to live in the house, bringing with them their own detail of living, like the fellow who played Elvis' albums for an hour each evening, and one time a woman who'd flush the toilet before and after using it; all irritating habits, yet comfort to be had from the picture forming of that person. From the number of tights which gathered there each week, I knew, for instance, that this woman worked as either a shop assistant or had a job in an office: factory girls don't wear skirts. I never actually saw her face, only the top of her head as she bobbed up to the street door each evening around six.

From then on there was always a pair of tights or two on that line. I would push them roughly to one side when taking my shower, leaving them all bunched up. Angry. Sitting, pissing, I would be aware of them, like a shadow: a dull feeling on the mind, making the small room feel even smaller. I'd laugh at myself. Nervously. Soon, even in my room, I'd be haunted by the anger and nervousness: an incubating rage. It was with me everywhere. Once, I woke up in the middle of the night feeling that I'd just lost something vital, like a key. But it was only a dream. It was a Saturday night. I could have been out there with the intermittent shrieks of laughter, the tell-tale scrape of high-heels and the muffled thump-thump call of drum-beat pulsing out into the night from a pub down that street. I ached, tired I thought. 'Choice' is the word I chose with which to lighten myself. 'Choice' I am here in this room. 'Choice' I am alone here in this room. 'Choice' I am alone here in this room on a Saturday night. 'Choice'. The feeling from the dream persisted, pestering me. I eyed the room, seeking in the dark the familiar, feeling its size: searching.

It is dawn. The revellers dispersed. The world quiet. I am sitting on the bathroom floor, knees tucked to my chin, back against the wall. From the clothes-line a pair of tights hang, knotted by both toes – spread-leg: the birth position: the sex position. Treacherous act. My act.

'Just to see,' I say, waking again from that dream on that night. I trot to the bathroom, knot the tights, slide them to their spread-leg – female – position. I stand back to see them. I see them.

Treacherous act. My father's. I am fifteen years old. The tights are off-white. My tights. My school tights. On the line they hang. Toes knot-bound and parted. Ominous. Lustful. His thrill. My threat. Six months later, I left. And they were there, still, as he had placed them. Undisturbed.

'Just to see,' I say, closing the bathroom door on my treacherous act. I slept.

She left. Two weeks later she was gone. I saw her load her stuff into a taxi one Friday evening, bobbing quickly from the street door to the taxi. Thump! The boot of the car closing.

Thump! The passenger door closed. It smelt of stale cigarette smoke and pine air freshener. My heart was pounding. As though I'd just run a race. He, the taxi driver, was pacing about the road, a cigarette dangling from the corner of his mouth.

'I'm ready,' I said, partially rolling down the window.

'And the road? Where does it lead to?'

'It's a dead-end,' I tell him. 'There's nothing down there, except a lake. It has a picnic area.'

'No! Is that a fact? That's a fine place,' he continued, nodding in the direction of the big house across the road.

'Healy's. Solicitors. Both of them.' I was used to saying that.

'Is that a fact!' The car moved forward.

'I'll turn here.' He swung the car into Healy's gateway, stopping just short of the gate. The house, one of indiscriminate size and shape, sat there. Alien windows. Blind windows. Up the road we drove, passing the row of cottages on our right. Some having rectangular extensions of bathrooms and back kitchens. Familiar windows. Squinting windows. Holding in their panes the reflection of the high stone wall which was on the other side of the road. It was not on these I looked. Instead I allowed my eyes to be raked by the flashing bodies of the trees beyond the wall.

Choice. I had had none. That's what I learned at twenty-one.

It was a shock: the tights, my action, the memory, her leaving. It was too much. The coincidence, too, of my sudden friendlessness. It was as though they all knew I was a pervert. In the canteen at work I sat alone. Proud and aloof, they thought; defensive and vulnerable, the reality; self-distrustful and confused, the truth, the deep truth.

I took to reading, not having done so since I was young. It had been Enid Blyton before, it was Agatha Christie then. One and the same to me: nice people in a nice world with no room for the baddies. I loved their manners and their houses and what they had to eat. Christie's summing up was always essential for me, for I could never figure out who had done the terrible deed. And, like Blyton, there were so many books. There was something comforting in that, in the number of books to be read by the same author. I'd go to Easons, usually on Saturday evening, walk to the same row of shelves, and there they'd be, the familiar row of books. I'd scan the titles and make my choice. I read those books at work, during the lunch break. Alone and aloof. Initially they, my workmates, came over to where I sat, handled the book.

'God! How'd you read that stuff?'

The covers of those books were usually gruesome: blood-stained dagger or body with a bullet wound in the back of the skull.

'You shouldn't judge a book by its cover.' My voice sounded stupid to my own ears. Others asked if there was any 'spice' in my books. I reddened. They laughed.

My routine changed just a little. Instead of going dancing, I read a lot, walked a lot, watched a lot from my window. I opened a savings account. Bought a bolt for my door. Had curtains made for the window: good ones; heavy ones. Curtains that darkened the room entirely, day or night.

A year passed.

A month before the Krups' social, he sat beside me one lunchtime.

'Hercule Poirot's little grey cells are winning through, I suppose?' These were the first words he ever spoke to me.

'No. Actually it's Miss Marple's knitting needles for a change.'

'Well, we definitely cannot accuse Christie of sexism, can we?' He laughed. I laughed. I didn't really understand what he meant, being as much confused by him as by my flirt-type response.

'Bill Ryan. Stores. A Galway man.' He offered me his hand.

I took it. Held it.

'Elizabeth Wallace. Assistant supervisor. Limerick, with an overlay of Kerry.' I let his hand go. We laughed again. I wriggled. We talked some more. Small talk. That kind of talk which doesn't really matter, an excuse to stay looking at each other, gauging one's impression on the other, eyes smiling, searching, mouths smiling, questioning. I don't recall how the conversation ended, remembering only that I felt lost when he was gone.

I couldn't wait to finish work that day, couldn't wait to be alone with this new happening. I bought a take-away. I couldn't eat it. Cups of tea steamed on my window seat, cooling quickly in the time lapse of my fantasising, a shock to the lips when sipped. Slopped in the sink and yet another cup made. I scrambled an egg and made some toast.

'I always like something light in the evenings,' I said aloud. I was speaking to him, in a future time, in a future place and he was speaking to me. I smoked and nodded and said 'Yes' to the words he spoke to me from that place. In dreams there is no shame. I lay on my bed, fully clothed. The room street-bright, cosy-amber diluted occasionally by the lights of passing cars. On my side I lay, my arm about my waist: his.

I arrived at work earlier than usual the following morning, chose a discreet spot in the foyer, and scanned the crowd of workers as they arrived. Cars came, moving and choosing like a colourful colony of monster-size birds, perching eventually in a space. From them many shapes and sizes emerged, but none was his. I did not see him at lunchtime, but later in the afternoon I did see him sauntering through a nearby aisle, a bunch of multi-coloured papers in his hand. I watched others watch him as he passed.

The following morning I focused my attention on the main gate, where those who bussed it, walked or cycled it filed through, a mass of bodies through which the cars crawled. He was there amongst them, two companions flanking him. He was entertaining them with some tale, smiling and nodding as he spoke, his hands stuffed in the pockets of his bomber jacket, elbows tucked like wings at his side. I was hiding by the side of the security hut. I hoped I'd meet him at lunchtime, but didn't. I was disappointed but not despairing. That evening I loitered in the bicycle shelter by the main gate, waiting for him to pass. He did so, alone. He was heading towards Jamesboro', my route to the bedsit.

My heart pounded and palms sweated as I walked some distance behind him, just one more factory girl in that crowd of factory girls chattering homewards in our navy-blue overalls. Down William Street he went, the factory crowd thinning. He passed my flat. I passed my flat, promising myself that I'd go no farther than Burton's corner. I'd turn back. Forget it. But I kept going. Finally, I stopped at Sarsfield Bridge, watching him as he walked on, expecting him to walk out along the Ennis Road. But he didn't. He turned right at the end of the bridge, continuing down along Clancy's Strand. I rushed halfway across the bridge, my eyes following his every movement. He stopped outside a house with a maroon-coloured door. In he went, the door flapping at his presence. It was a gem of knowledge: I knew where he lived! I hugged myself with the delight of it all. I rushed back to the bedsit, showered, washed my hair and dressed to go out, which I did later that evening.

Down Patrick Street I walked, coming soon to the bridge under which the Abbey river flows. I stopped there, looking at this river pouring itself into the Shannon; murky water the colour of weak, unmilked tea. Across the rushing spread of the Shannon I could see the house on Clancy's Strand. So close! On I walked. Past an open space to my left, a dead-end, the courthouse and other buildings flanking this space. Up and on I go under the trees of St Mary's cathedral, turning left at the top of the short hill. Moving along, more easily then, by the high walls of the old city, shiny and worn in places, like a church waterfont. Nicholas Street, a poor street, footpath narrow, street narrow, bars without lounges, all the shops were small shops, proclaiming bargains in carpets, furniture, food, signs written on electric-green or electric-orange-coloured posters in dirty windows, the hand-writing self-consciously trailing down in size from its bold beginnings. Past King John's castle with houses for the poor in its courtyard. Rounding its round base at the start of Thomond Bridge, a Shannon bridge, I hear the first river-rumblings of the Shannon as it funnels through the seven arches of that bridge. The wind there was unexpected, exhilarating though, booming in my ears, mingling with the river noise, together a thunder.

Halfway across I stopped. I looked. I could see the house on Clancy's Strand. On I walked, briskly, invigorated by the wind and the noise and the newness of the place. I'd not been to that part of town before. The flat head of the Treaty Stone came into view, resting as it did at the end of the bridge. It has been moved since that time, an obstruction to traffic it had become. My pace became a strolling pace as I self-consciously ambled along Clancy's Strand, my attention firmly fixed on the Shannon's rushing waters. There's a low wall between the river and the road, perfect for sitting on, which I did after passing the house with the maroon-coloured door. I smiled to myself, acknowledging the cheek of my chase.

'Well! Well! Well! What a small world!' I'd planned to say that if I happened to meet *anybody*. I would smile while saying it, I planned, continuing with something like: 'Galway doesn't have anything as beautiful as this' – no: 'spectacular' would be better – 'Galway doesn't have anything as spectacular as this.' Would I say Bill, or would I say Mr Ryan just for the fun of it? I would tell him that I always came over here of an evening, that I found it relaxing.

I met no one, no one at all. But I wasn't disappointed. I mean, it was a long-shot after all. I retraced my steps, briskly. And just as I reached the Treaty Stone again, I saw him, as clear as day. He came out of the bar across the street, The Treaty Bar. I stood stock still, reversed quickly to the cover of the Treaty Stone and hid myself from view. I could see him clearly though. He was wearing a beautiful red-check shirt under his bomber jacket. I'd not seen him dressed like that before. He looked really well. He was alone. He walked along the strand wall, not stopping until he was directly across from the house with the maroon-coloured door. He straddled the wall like you'd straddle a horse, his face bent to the river for some moments.

I could have fainted. I mean, I would simply have died a death if I'd met him there a few moments before. The shock of it made me shiver. I turned on my heels and took flight – running and stumbling and stopping and running again, people gaping after me as I passed on my crazy dash. Exhausted, I stopped and leaned against a wall, pulling hard and fast for air, gradually my breathing becoming slower and easier, until finally I had it under control. I was trembling all over, shock-cold, elated and relieved. A snort of laughter escaped from me, like the half-bark of a retreating dog. Another one followed, like a hiccup, then another and another, building together despite my struggle to smother them – it, a scream of cry-laughter, wide-mouth and throaty, uncontrollable. People stopped and looked, I'm sure, but I saw nothing.

Next day was Friday. I avoided the canteen, feeling angry. To hell with him, I thought, why should I put myself out just because of him? Stuck-up bastard; he probably didn't like me anyway – not in that way, he probably felt sorry for me, sitting there on my own, maybe even someone dared him to go over to me, just for the laugh, just for the skit – that was probably it all right; a fellah like that probably had a girlfriend, probably back in Galway – it was all the one to me; I mean, why should I care? I mean, he only sat talking to me for no more than a quarter of an hour or so; there's no big deal in that.

I saw them in Moran's shop window on my way back from the launderette that Saturday: three different-coloured check shirts, blue-check, green-check and red-check like his. The green one was dressing the headless and armless torso of a mannequin, the others square-folded still and fanned out like a hand of playing cards. I went into the shop. I chose a green one. Back at the bedsit I tried it on immediately. It went with my colouring. It went with my jeans, tucked inside or not. I tucked it in again, let it hang out again. It looked really well. I'd never been as pleased with an outfit before. The whole thing would be set off with a leather belt, I giggled at the thought. Out the door, down the stairs, into the street, back to the shop to buy a belt. I chose a brown one with a floral design etched all over it. My fingers fumble-feeding it through the loops, the assistant uncertain of how to proceed, gaping at me with my fiver in his hand. I said: 'I'll wear it, no need to wrap it.' He handed me my change, saying: 'It looks well.' I could tell he was embarrassed. I giggled in reply. I felt good. On my way up that Saturday evening street, I stopped to look in the shop windows, an excuse to admire my reflection.

There's a Chinese restaurant on that street. No one I'd ever known had been in there. If I'm not mistaken, I believe it was the first of its kind in the city. All tinted glass, variegate plastic plants, the jarring combination of red and green paintwork, its name written in that oriental squiggle, tapered and flattened and tapered again, a grave, golden lion gaping at you as you entered, and the smell: exotic or awful, it was hard to tell until you'd eaten the stuff. That evening I stopped to read the menu displayed in the window, concentrating on the take-away. I decided to try something 'vegetable', remembering the story that went around Limerick one time of how the Chinese used grey-hound instead of chicken in their dishes.

'Vegetable chop suey,' I ordered over-authoritatively.

'Flied rice. Biled rice. Which?' I thought her face beautiful, full and round, without freckle or blemish, eyes, nose and mouth perfectly set and hair of the deepest, darkest sheen.

I asked for boiled rice, perhaps because it was the one last mentioned. She motioned to a row of comfortable-looking chairs, one of which was occupied by a lady engrossed in her newspaper. I sat three chairs away from her, breathing deeply in order to prevent myself from laughing: me! in a place like this. And when I sat facing a large Chinese print depicting slim, white-faced Chinese women, all parasols, kimonos, ruby-red lips and tiny feet, an attitude of listening, presumably to the singing of the various birds in the scene, a hiccup of laughter escaped from me. I felt excited, elated in fact. I kept thinking: what am I doing in a place like this? I must be mad: or something.

Back at the bedsit, I emptied the contents of the foil containers onto two separate plates, smelling the rice before tasting it, then carefully examining the ingredients of the vegetable chop suey, the mushrooms and onion being the only vegetables I recognised. And all the while I was aware of my new shirt and how it looked and felt, tucked inside my jeans, and my belt, wrapped about my waist, a new sensation just above my hip bone. When I'd finished eating, I stood up to examine my reflection captured in the window of the bedsit. I noticed for the first time the cut of my jeans, felt how well they anticipated the contours of my body. I pressed the fanned fingers of both hands over the back pockets, checking for folds created there by the bulk of the shirt tucked inside the jeans, moving slowly over my hips, tips of fingers pressing, checking the slight camber of my stomach, thumbs closing in on the taper of my waist, hands crossing over at that point, continuing their caress until meeting the trapped roll of bra-flesh, hands crossing over again, fingers lingering on the pockets of the shirt, they were buttoned, the pockets; finger-fumbled, they opened, fingers dipped in, checking, noticing the faint fur of the material. Feeling.

I planned to wear that outfit to work the following week, but didn't, not having the guts to do so. I followed him home from work every evening, stopping halfway across Sarsfield Bridge, as I had done on that first evening. Some evenings, just as the street lights came on, I'd walk to the bridge over the Abbey river and watch the lights from the house with the maroon-coloured door. And once, I walked that block – Patrick Street, Rutland Street, left at the junction on Bridge Street, along Nicholas Street, swinging left again at King John's castle, then coming to Thomond Bridge, turning onto Clancy's Strand, skipping across Sarsfield Bridge like someone fleeing some unnamed night-dread, a giggle or scream bubbling under. And when he asked me, I could have been knocked sideways with a feather.

'You're not thinking of going to the social, are you?' We were in the canteen, my book winged out, face downwards between us, the cover showing a cracked skull in which a half-eaten, ruby-red, worm-infested apple was framed. It was a shock, pure and simple. I crossed my legs, squeezing my thighs tightly.

'Hadn't really thought about it, to be honest.' I was nonchalant and dying. I said: 'Are you?'

'I will, if you will.' He smiled. His upper lip twitched momentarily. Nervous.

'I haven't been to that since ... well it must be nearly two years at this stage. Perhaps it *is* time I went again.'

We both studied the cover of the book.

'Have you ever been?'

He told me that he'd only been working in Krups for a year and hadn't even thought of going to last year's social.

'In that case, why should I deprive you of a night out?'

We both laughed.

I phoned in sick for the next two days, the first time I'd ever done so in all my time there. I stayed in bed, thinking. Alternating between absolute bliss and disbelief, going over the conversation again and again, knowing it was true but doubting it at the same time, wanting to think beyond it but frightened, going back to it again, delighted. Light-headed, I peered through my window as he passed on his way home from work.

I had two weeks to prepare for the social, and it had been easy, except for my hair. The dress: long sleeves, high neck, low hem line, black; the shoes: flat, black. The hair needed trimming, I'd known that for ages, but had no one to do it for me. The eyebrow plucking, make-up try-outs and hair-trimming sessions were still a feature of Friday lunch-time in the factory, but you couldn't just barge into a group and ask for your hair to be trimmed. I knew I'd have to go to a hairdresser, an experience as alien and unwanted as choosing a coffin. There was a Peter Mark-type salon just down the street from me, all window, fashionable heads on fashionable bodies – beauty: yours for the asking. I believe if I could have imagined myself in there, I would have braved it. But I just couldn't. It seemed so laughable: me! in a place like that, with those fashionable young ones.

The place I chose was cramped but clean. Dated ladies smiled at me from posters on the wall, their smiles flanked by tusk-like kiss-curls. I was the first customer – early and anxious. The hairdresser wore a stiff, white, nylon overall, had a stiff, straight mouth, carrot-coloured curls. Her thinness deprived her of matronliness.

I said: 'But I only want a trim.'

She had asked me to sit by the sink.

'Well you see, Miss, wet hair cuts far easier than dry.' She was pleasant and persuasive. I yielded as she eased my head back. Eyes closed, I relaxed as the spray rained gently on my head, opening them when the spraying ceased, surveying the room from that angle. I closed them again as the cool blob of shampoo trickled on my scalp. And then it started, the kneading. I gasped.

'I'm not hurting you, am I?' She lifted her hands back from my head, gloved in suds, poised to start again.

'No. No. No.' I shifted in the seat.

'More comfortable now?'

I nodded. She continued. The pattern she traced on my head was familiar, churning up echoes of: 'Don't rub so hard, Mama, you're hurting me. The suds are getting in my eyes, Mama – my ears, Mama, don't let the water in my ears, Mama.' Then losing my head in the big blue bath towel, damp from the head that had gone before, vigorously tossed between firm fingers, the developing rhythm causing a rhythm – like rhythms do – in my body.

Back and forth I tossed my head, seeking those soothing fingertips, straining, aching, eyes shut tight.

'Are you okay?' I hear her ask.

'Is this going to take much longer?' I snapped.

Our night out was formal and false, but it was a start. We chatted, we danced, we ate, we drank. He told me I looked well. I said: 'I wish I had me jeans.' He said: 'Me too.' We smiled. We spoke of our bosses, pals and enemies within the factory.

'No chance they'd swap this for a pizza?' forking tongues of turkey around his plate. I said: 'Or a Fo Yung special.'

'Chinese? I've never tried it.'

I'd never had pizza, but I didn't say so.

It was time to dance, and so we did. The fast set first, indifferent to each other, so conscious were we as we danced, he mouthing the words of the song, I staring interestedly at a point beyond his head. Once, he moved in close to me, placed both his hands on my shoulders: 'It's so strange to see everyone in their best clothes.' He sprang back from me, continuing his observations.

The slow set came: we returned to our table after a detour to the bar by him and a detour to the cloakroom by me. We sipped our drinks and chatted our chat, performed our laughter during the antics of the spot-prize interlude, applauded seriously the manager's speech. We took to the floor again for the final slow set, our hands colliding – like boxers – in the confusion over where to place them on each other's body. We laughed. My hands came to rest on his shoulders, his found their way to my waist, more or less resting on the place where my new leather belt would sit. He trembled, slightly. From over his shoulder I could see a dancing couple probing their tongues in each other's mouth, her hands gripping his arse. They, in their blindness, collided with us, causing our bodies to press together. My body flowed with his as he detached himself.

You could say he was a very ordinary type of person,

medium height and build, pale eyes, fair hair and a winning smile in an attractive face. The youngest of seven. Brothers and sisters living in New York, London and Dublin, a good Inter- and Leaving Cert from the Christian Brothers, parents struggling the struggle they'd always struggled on twenty-five acres of Galway land, fearing their future alone.

He said: 'If I didn't leave, they'd become too dependent on me – I'd be stuck with them.'

He went home every weekend, to play football or hurling or something like that.

'Just to keep in touch with old friends there. You know how it is?'

He shared a house in Limerick with two others, both of whom worked permanent nights in a factory in Shannon.

'I don't ever really get to see them, but I can live with that.'

His was a happy nature, one who could laugh at the misfortunes of others. Cripples amused him, yet cripples liked him.

'You should have seen the jaw on this fellow I met the other night in the pub!'

His ability to describe deformity was impressive, his amusement genuine and infectious. He would then tell the tale told by that person, usually amusing, seldom boring, often personal. I would listen, usually amused, seldom bored, occasionally perturbed, nodding my interest, smiling my amusement, concealing the rest. And on he'd prattle, engrossed in the story of that person.

The photos of home came. Blurred, bent, precious, black and white evidence of a time unremembered: bundle of new baby held by proud parents, shy and stiff; bundle of new baby held by an older child – 'That's me being held by my sister.' Then Santa Claus photos, communion photos, school photos, confirmation photos.

In the background of most was the house, door open, cat on the sill, bicycle or bucket by the wall, geraniums filling the window, a dog watching on; there were aunts and uncles in summery style, calling for their summer Sunday visit, men in sleeves rolled past the elbow, women in dresses, flowery and cool. A potted history of all; the childless aunt who had a roomful of baby clothes; the alcoholic uncle, minty and fun, but with a sad-looking wife, nervous and cutting.

'But we understand.'

His parents: strict, hardworking, life not to be evaluated in terms of happiness or sadness – just work; a beast to be bought, a drain to be dug, a barn to be built; cows milked, calved and cleaned, hay cut, turned and saved, children fed, washed and schooled, the house clean, basic and bare; they believed in Hell, hoped for Heaven and feared the priest.

'They worked so hard all their lives they never had time to be bad.'

There was a photo of his brother, the eldest, five years in Maynooth, a prison officer now in Mountjoy. This photo had been enlarged; it was of him in uniform, and a copy of it stood on the mantelpiece in his mother's kitchen.

Then a photo of two of his sisters in nursing white, smiles caring and bright, a colour photo from London. And colour photos of the three in New York, two brothers that worked on the buildings, grinning their smiles in some New York pub; they were working and studying; and his sister, alone on a park bench, her smile direct and seductive, almost private, a waitress, taking night classes in something or other.

And this is their wedding photo: his parents, again. October 1953 – the hay was in, the cows were in calf, the time was right. He told me that his mother's waist was the same width as the leg of his father's wedding trousers.

'They were both pushing on.'

She left her mother to her brother on fifteen acres; this is the uncle whose life he would not copy. She, his grand-mother, lived to the age of ninety-seven.

'My uncle was tied to her, and when she died he was too bitter to care about anything – even himself.'

He had all their stories, his parents' stories. He had packed them with his own and carried them everywhere. He had the history of that community, in their yarns and their tales. He spoke familiarly of persons long dead, whom he'd never known; he was complete in his knowledge, knowing the awfulness of real people, understanding the role of circumstance and fate in their lives; knowing that Bessy Clifford buried her unwanted babies in the dung heap, knowing that Bessy Clifford's husband had had his first epileptic fit a month before their marriage. She had one baby. She took a chance. It was a boy. He was okay. She out-lived her husband by fifteen years. Mr Clifford had drowned in a nearby river, presumably as a result of one of his seizures. Bessy Clifford had lived out her remaining years, alone. By then her story was complete; she'd been the pitied bride, the murderous bitch, the token mother. Their son became a priest. During the years he'd spent in the seminary, his parents were avoided by everyone: such an offering God would surely refuse. Bessy Clifford and her husband worked seven days a week to pay the fees, never asking the favours their neighbours were all set to refuse.

'Who'd have thought?' they said, on the day of the ordination.

At her husband's funeral they shook her hand, saying: 'We're sorry for your troubles.' He said: 'She was then thin, like themselves, old and world-weary. Most of them would have seen their own compromise with virtue along the way.'

He had many other tales like that one, a whole community of tales. A tale of a school friend, full of fun and devilment, hell-bent on high-jinks, parents driven distracted.

'His grandfather was the very same. He's supposed to have cycled the entire length of the railway bridge wall: drunk.'

He'd been told that tale by his father. And his mother

warned him to stay away from those Walsh girls.

'She never said why, but I found out when I was fourteen.'

He had been to their homes, the homes in his community, helping at hay-time or cutting turf, tasting their hospitality and hearing their tales.

He had seen their dead. Seven years old on seeing his first corpse. It was an accident; he'd been told to stay outside in the kitchen with the other children, given a bag of Taytos and a mineral as the bribe, but curiosity got the better of him.

'From a child's point of view, there was nothing to see: an old man asleep in a box called a coffin means nothing to a seven-year-old. It was the adults who had the dread. Parents! They'd make you laugh.'

They came to his house, to pass the time, to share the news, to share trouble and fear over stock, weather, sons, daughters, venting anger over temporary foes, seeking vindication; quick to argue, fast bursts of indignation, sharpened in rehearsal, diluted by nervousness and the past.

'It was serious, but it wasn't, if you know what I mean.' I didn't, but I didn't say so.

Being the youngest, he was aware while growing up of being sibling and son. There was always a brother or sister taking him somewhere by the hand, or on the carrier or cross-bar of a bicycle, to school, to mass, to the bog, to visit cousins on a Sunday, or for ice cream on a hot day, to fish, to rob orchards, to fight off rival gangs. When any of his sisters were going for a stroll of an evening, his mother always insisted they take him along for the walk: an unwitting chaperon.

'I've to laugh when I think of it – they must have hated me.'

He was sent with his brothers, too, on such evening strolls, his mother threatening to kill him if he didn't tell her if they'd been smoking, and his brothers threatening to kill

49

him if he did.

'Their threat was more real than hers.'

Football matches were the outings he had with his father, outings his father had not taken since he married. The day started with a leg-numbing ride on the cross-bar of his father's bicycle to the railway station, sandwiches and a flask rolled in the top coat on the back carrier, the promise of Taytos and a mineral once they got to the station kept him patient with the numbness in his leg. They met others along the way, all packing together on the train, men and boys, fathers with sons, uncles with older nephews, brothers together, neighbours together, men on their own teaming up with other men on their own. He remembered it all so well; their endless conversation on the match, sober and spirited in anticipation, tight with the delight of victory, fighting drunk in the face of defeat, a giddy bicycle ride home regardless of the outcome.

'All the world knew my father, that's how it felt. "Is that your young fellah?" they'd ask, patting my head. "Yes," my father answered, "and I've two more at home minding the place for the day".'

I could picture the place where he lived; I could see it. Stone walls, scattered houses, a community straddling two ages: dun donkeys dragging bright-orange carts of turf, of silver milk tankards, of potatoes, of bent old men in black; red-bodied tractors resting in yards beside outhouses which were once dwelling houses, galvanised sheeting replacing the thatch, windows boarded and blind, the new bungalow nearby, taking with it the rick of turf, the black and white sheep-dog going with the rick, its house having always been built into it.

'The bungalows are grand, but there's nothing to beat the old houses. I remember coming home from school on a May evening and seeing a neighbour's house having been transformed with whitewash and a paintbrush. You don't see that any more.'

He lived in the house his grandfather had built, a modern farmhouse instead of a bungalow.

'Bungalows have door-bells, farmhouses have latches.'

There was a church, grey, central, protected by towering yews. He wasn't a believer.

'Not really.'

He went there every Sunday, accepting the acknowledgement of his elders, transferring gradually from that group of males who gathered together at the gate to discuss the match and the dance, to the one that discussed men in power, the match and the health of parents.

'They stopped calling me "young Ryan" a long time ago.'

He drank with them on Saturday nights, his father always standing him the first pint, proudly.

'He never had the chance to do so with the others.'

There was music in the pub of a Saturday night, an aged hippy plucking a guitar, singing Bob Dylan and Simon and Garfunkel songs. The hippy was there especially to entertain all the young people back from the cities for the weekend.

'He wears the same tie-dyed T-shirt every week, sings the same songs and tells the same jokes.'

He recalled the pride he had felt as a child on arriving home with a silken crow feather for his father, a gift with which he cleaned the stem of his pipe; or the delight of his mother when he arrived back on a June evening, presenting her with a sprig of strongly scented honeysuckle.

'It was a ritual passed down from one to the other.'

He told me the tale of the day he knew he was an adult. He was ten at the time. It was summer. He was at his bachelor uncle's farm, helping with the hay-making. A number of his cousins were there also. It was hot, hard work.

'He worked us like men, having no understanding of children.'

A feature of his uncle's farm were the cats, a colony of multi-coloured, wild cats, all shapes and sizes, fierce-looking toms and even fiercer-looking queens, prowling, preying, scary silhouettes on a moonlit night, basking, balled up in the sunshine, spitting and clawing when disturbed, giving as much fright as being frightened, fleeing to the heights which they reigned, proudly preening themselves on windowsills, their narrow pink tongues moistening curved paws which they pulled over long whiskers and pointed ears. The farmyard was like any other: stony and potholed. In one of the potholes rested the hubcap of a car wheel, and into this his uncle slopped a splash of milk on his way in from milking the cows. To it the cats scurried, their bellies touching the ground: stalkers in for the kill.

'It was the only food they were ever given by anyone. My uncle made out they'd never be ratters if they were too well-fed.'

Himself and his uncle were returning to the fields one day after their midday meal; his five-year-old cousin was also with them. On the kitchen windowsill sat a cat, regal and wary.

'What's his name?' asked the cousin. 'The uncle came out with "Percy", straight out without stopping to think. It was so funny. I looked at my uncle, and do you know what he did? He winked at me!'

That was it; that was his story of adult initiation: a story about a man with a cat that wasn't called Percy.

We used to meet on Wednesday evening, by the bridge at half-past seven. We would walk, everywhere, anywhere, neither of us really deciding on where we'd go. He'd point in a certain direction, and off we'd walk; I'd choose a street or two along the way and he'd agree. We held hands, linked arms, walked and talked, and as the evening darkened we'd find a pub and have a drink. Kiss goodnight. Spring passed; summer passed; winter came.

'And you?' he asked

This direct attention confounded me; I giggled and

reddened and blinked, struck poses of thoughtfulness, saying things like: 'Gee, I don't know' or 'Gee, I never thought about that.' Later, alone, I would sweat with embarrassment, calling myself a fool, not thinking of his question, only of my behaviour. He had a story of mine; the part which was like his own.

I left home to work in the city.

'A bit like yourself,' I said.

'The same here,' I said to his fear of being stuck with ageing parents. I had neither the good Inter nor Leaving but I had the experience of two years with the nuns, so I lied about the Inter, though only to make things look neater, a natural break as it were.

'We had this Sister Rose,' I said, 'small and thin, with a red, wet tip to her nose. We had her for Christian Doctrine. She made us laugh with her sweeping walk.' I'm sure he matched that teacher-tale with one of his own, but I forget it now.

As he was the youngest, I was the eldest; he and I were the same age.

'Old bossy-boots, I suppose.'

He could imagine the rows between four sisters, the teasing over boyfriends, the jealously over figures, the disputes over clothes, the togetherness behind it all. He'd seen it himself.

'I've no surprises for you so.'

'Would you like to have had a brother?'

'No.'

My parents' history I simply did not know. My mother came from Kerry; how she ended up in Limerick I never found out. My father, a Limerick man, had worked as a farm labourer until the building boom of the 1960s, eventually taking a job in one of the factories on which he'd laboured. I don't know how they had met; she never spoke of a grand romance.

'They were probably like my own.'

53

He knew she was dead. He didn't probe; not then.

He asked: 'How?'

'A fire.'

'I'm sorry. Your house, was it?'

'A neighbour's. It isn't always easy to ...'

'I know! I know! I'm sorry.'

That usually worked for me.

'Why a bedsit?'

'What do you mean?'

'Why not share with some others – for the company?'

'Gee! I never thought of that.'

It was the first of those questions, those disquieting questions. Later, I sat through the night on that bedsit window, facing into that street-lit room. Friday night. It was party night, and all the sounds of a partying world were just outside my door: shrieks of laughter, choruses started but never finished, speeding cars, motor-bikes, troops of males, noisy, belligerent, without mates, car doors closing, street doors closing, into the house it came, the fumble of keys in locks, suppressed laughter, curses, thump! thump! thump! up the stairs, past my door, thump! thump! thump! down the stairs, past my door, the clink of bottles from the room below, the hum of a radio from the room above, laughter, words, silences, the smell of chips and alcohol gathering in the hallway, seeping into my room.

I go to the bathroom, climbing the stairs slowly. Someone from the floor above tries the door while I'm in there.

'There's someone in there,' I hear him say to his companions – or companion – before closing the door above. I smile.

At four in the morning the street is deserted, the house is settling, footsteps are quieter, voices too. The front door is eased shut. I look to the street and see a man moving catlike, quick but cautious, on his way. Friday night.

Friday night. Fish night of old.

They were always on the kitchen table when I arrived home from school on Friday. Herrings: blue-black and silver, belly to back on a plate, gutted, with flaps of flesh folding together like mouths without teeth. Fried they'd be, served without sauce or ceremony. She'd be sitting by the range, fat, asleep – why should Friday be any different! No welcome. No argument. Nothing, but a sleep-snarled face. I'd wash up the breakfast cups and then wash the spuds, three for each of us, five for our father. O! She'd be awake all right. I knew that. Her sleep wasn't a true sleep. It was something worse: it was inertia and apathy rolled into one. I know that now. But then I thought it was a game, one of those I'm-pretending-not-to-be-watching-just-to-see-if-you'll-be-good games. Sometimes I'd talk to her, telling her about my day at school, reasonable stuff, like who got slapped and why, who was absent and why, what the teacher wore. Mostly there was no response, although I'd sometimes catch her following me with half-open eyes. On and on I'd babble like any child does to inanimate things, dolls or kittens or stones with faces, either animal or human, the tale becoming more fantastic, full of the freedom of a child's imagination, unchecked and awful, searching for reality or something.

She said: 'You're a terrible little liar, d'you know that? No one can believe a word that comes out of that mouth of yours.'

Friday night. Fear night.

On the stroke of the Angelus she'd know her fate: he'd be drunk, he'd be late. She'd be cruel and silent in her dread, busily venting her anger on dishes that needed washing, on floors that needed sweeping; I'd be nodded at and prodded at to do this, that and the other: the slave-stuff of childhood. She'd kick schoolbags and shoes from corners, scattering books and newspapers to the kitchen floor, a pile of anger gathering there, around which she danced. She raged through bedrooms, beds made in double-quick time, a flight of feathers left floating in the air. We'd scurry from one safe corner to the next, like sheep scattering.

Sometimes he'd be very late. She'd have nothing left to do but sit, watch, listen, arms folded across her belly and tucked beneath her breasts. Around the kitchen we'd sit like watchers at a wake; silent, like watchers at a wake; fearful, like watchers at a wake.

The television is off; she wants to hear him coming.

So there we'd sit, five souls, five female souls in the hellish-red, whorish-red glow of the sacred heart lamp, with a fish for our father in the oven, waiting for our fate that is our father.

Friday night. Fist night.

It never mattered whether he came home early or late, whether we'd see them or not, whether we'd be asleep or not; they'd row and fight and argue: he'd hit her – one, two, three, just like Muhammad Ali. On Friday night she'd lie beside me, weeping.

Saturday morning. The reek of alcohol and herrings, up-ended dannos by the range. I'd be the first one up, roused by her to draw the curtains: a mask of normality for the neighbours, like her smile. Later, the place dull and crowded with the two of them, she aimless in her hurt and hate, hiding; our father, hunched by the range, smoking, coughing, hawking.

Saturday morning. The street lights have long since been out, allowing real light its reign. It is that time, dawn but not day. The house is still. Asleep. I have come to know this place so well. Soon they will rise, radios will hum, water will flush and flow, doors will open and close, close and open, like some crazy stage farce. I'll smell morning. Bathroom steam – soapy and balmy; someone's fry-up – salty and tempting. One by one they'll leave. Back to their homes, back to the boyfriend, back to the girlfriend, back with their dirty laundry.

I strip naked, for it is time to sleep. I need to go to the toilet. I rush out as I am, smiling as I sit there on the bowl, feeling silly and safe. Feeling sillier and safer, I stand on the landing, unfolding my arms from across my naked breasts. It is so peaceful. I place my foot on the stair-step leading to the next landing, springing lightly, as light as one can be only when naked. I stop there to look from the window, surveying the view from over the head of the Virgin sitting on the windowsill, a world of ugly rooftops, old slates, rusty galvanise, new slates. I wave my fanned fingers through the cobwebs stretching from the statue's prayer-clasped hands to its chin. On I go to the top floor, passing other doors, other worlds behind them, pausing briefly at each one, brave in my nakedness. Down to the front door I fly, naked feet padding along like a cat's. I press myself against the door, feeling stings of cold air jetting against my body. I am sleepy, really sleepy. I run up to my room, pull the curtains together, making dark.

We met that night. I said: 'A bedsit's not a bad place.'

I bought a pot plant, all arched tongues of green and cream. It hung before the window from a hook in the ceiling. It flourished there, producing long stems, from the ends of which fresh saplings appeared.

Family. If you run from it, if you must run from it, if you hide, disguise, pretend, select, if your soliloquy is not a happy one, then you are dumb: until the torrent comes. Childhood is family. Family is possession: *my* mother, *my* father, *my* brother, *my* sister, *my* wife, *my* husband, *my* house, *my* room, *my* kitchen, *my* bed, *my* daughter, *my* son. My family. You honour it all. Happy talk or no talk at all. Lies are not lies when you're honouring thy father and thy mother:

'He was never bad to us.'

'She had her troubles.'
'They had their difficulties.'
'We didn't go hungry.'
'She was never bad to us.'
'He had his troubles.'
'They had their difficulties.'
'We were hungry but happy.'

Wife! Honour thy husband.

If Birdie Geary hadn't sent that baseball bat home from America.

Husband! Honour thy wife.
'Her nerves get the better of her sometimes.'
Love-lies? Honour-lies? Family-lies?
Family lies.
My mother died in a fire, a fire in a neighbour's house: my family lie. Not just my lie. It was my family's family-lie.

One evening, one of those I-must-rush-to-meet-him evenings, he wasn't there.
I crossed the bridge expecting to meet him, thinking he was simply late. I did not meet him. When I reached the house with the maroon-coloured door, I concealed myself behind a lamp-post. I was anticipating pleasure, the pleasure of seeing someone rush from a house, door banging behind him as he rushed down steps, struggling into his jacket, rushing to meet me. I giggled. Nothing. I waited. Nothing. I panicked. The door opened to my knock. He said: 'Oh!' I said: 'Are you all right?'
'Am! Yeah.'
'You forgot it was Wednesday. Right?'
'Yeah! Wednesday. Right.'
'I do believe, Mr Ryan, that the little grey cells are starting to deteriorate.' The sweat tingled in my armpits. He

smiled. I smiled. I said: 'It'll be our little secret. Okay?'

'Do you want to come in, or what?'

I nodded.

The house he lived in was like any that's being rented for a long period of time: old-fashioned furniture, threadbare carpet, the smell of gas fumes. He made tea, then sat silent, cuddling his cup in his hands. I got him talking. I knew how to do that. I said: 'How was the weekend?' And that was that. Off he went on his usual route around his home place: the family, the church, the match, the pub afterwards, the cows, the health of his parents, how his brothers and sisters were getting on. And I was happy. When the conversation flagged, I drew on even more names with which I'd become familiar: Quinn, with the limp; Kelly, with a glass eye focused on Heaven; a myriad of characters with ever-changing dilemmas: births, marriages, deaths, new hostilities, new cars, new windows, new extensions, new relationships.

'And you?'

He knew I never went home at weekends.

He once said: 'Things can't be all that bad at home, surely?'

'You know how it is!'

'I suppose it's not the same without your mother.' I said nothing.

I told him about the book I was reading, *A Passage to India*. He'd not heard of it. So I told him all about Dr Aziz, an Indian doing his best to like the British, about his English friend Mr Fielding, a teacher who stands by him when things go wrong; about Mrs Moore and her son Ronny who is to marry Adela Quested, and how she accuses Aziz of 'interfering' with her while alone in the Marabar caves, the place where he had taken her and Mrs Moore on an outing – all train and elephants and baskets of food and commotion. And how the British reacted after the incident, and then how Mrs Moore believed Aziz was innocent, and how Miss

Quested withdrew her allegation, and didn't marry Ronny; about the sun and the heat and then the rain, and the big festival – much colour and noise. I finished.

'And what happened?'

'That's what happened.'

'Oh!'

'You'd have to read it to see.'

I thought of telling him the house was nice, comfortable. But I didn't. I didn't want any talk about houses or flats.

'You make good tea.'

'D'you want another cup?'

'No.'

There was silence, lots of long silence. He yawned. I left. We kissed at the doorway. The usual kiss, bodies apart, sealed lips meeting sealed lips. I once tried in the beginning to put my tongue in his mouth; I'd been embarrassed when he pulled away, laughing.

'Elizabeth!'

I was halfway down the steps, on my way, still in the glow of the light from the hallway. I turned. He skipped down to me, enfolded me in his arms, kissed my neck.

'I'm sorry, Elizabeth. I am really sorry.' I pushed him from me, laughing.

'Don't be such a fool, Billy. It's okay.' I scurried across the bridge, smiling, mumbling to myself. I said: 'What a fool! What a silly fool.'

It didn't matter when he wasn't at the usual place at the usual time the following week. The door opened to my knock.

'Elizabeth!'

He sounded different. I said nothing. Eventually he asked me in. He made tea. Sometime during that evening he asked: 'How did you know where I live?'

'You told me.' It was a lie. 'Don't you remember?'

'No.'

He didn't kiss me goodnight.

The following week the door didn't open to my knock. The sweat tingled in my armpits. I crossed the street, sat on the wall by the river. Waited. It was cold. Dark. Two hours later I saw him huddle down the footpath. I didn't hide. I was cold, a stiffening breeze coming off the river. I wanted him to see me there, I wanted him to see how cold I was. He didn't. He never looked up.

'Elizabeth!'

It was the morning after my vigil by the river. I was in the storeroom – his storeroom at work. His face reddened. I sneezed.

'Proof as to why I couldn't turn up last night.' I sneezed again, then laughed with tear-streaming eyes. I said: 'Am I forgiven?' The sweat tingled in my armpits.

'Am! Yeah! Sure!'

Again I sneezed; I had to spend some time blowing my nose. He was watching me all the while.

'There's nothing worse than having a cold.' I didn't give him a chance to speak. 'Duty calls. I'll see you again. By-e.'

On Monday night I walked that block, Patrick Street, Thomond Bridge, on to Clancy's Strand, trudging weakly and wearily on my way, wary on arriving at the house with the maroon-coloured door. I didn't stop. I didn't care. I didn't see him. I walked that block again on Tuesday night. On Wednesday morning I couldn't move, I felt weak all over. The cold I had was really slowing me down, and the pain I had with it was something else; it was in my head, in my stomach, my heart was racing and I kept crying, I hiccuped, my hands shook, I couldn't eat anything except chocolate, I couldn't sleep. I managed to get to the phone in the hallway, informing the foreman of my illness. Once back in the bedsit, I lay on my bed. I probably listened to the radio for a while, but I don't recall; I don't remember the type of day it was: cold, wet, windy or bright. I remember my pain. That's all. That's all you ever really remember. I washed my hair that evening and briefly felt better. An hour earlier than usual on

61

my usual Wednesday evening, I closed the door to the bedsit. I was dizzy. I was hot. I was cold. I stopped many times on my way to Clancy's Strand, leaning breathlessly against railings, signposts, buildings and bridges. Looking over the wall of the bridge, I could feel a stifling sensation rise up within me: I thought I would fall. Could fall. Just fall. Simply fall. Sucked forward by the solid-looking water, rushing, gurgling, flowing fast. Soft and solid. Like silk. To be wrapped in silk, cool, cool, silk. To sink in silk, in that cool silk.

'Are you okay there, Miss?'

I looked at the mouth that spoke. I could have cried.

The evening might have been wet, windy, calm, cold, mild, the street might have been busy or quiet, I might even have passed people I knew, but I don't recollect any of that. It was October. Early October, twilight at seven; late October, dark at seven: but I can't say which or whether. I was cold. I was hot. I was rushing. I was waiting.

I was waiting by the Treaty Stone, propped against it, facing the street to the house with the maroon-coloured door. Behind me was the Treaty Bar. My eyes told me lies, and every person passing was him. I called his name. I said: 'Bil-ly.' People looked on, then moved on. Soon, I knew, I would start walking in the direction of the house with the maroon-coloured door. Soon. Soon. Soon.

He said: 'Drink this.' The fringe of the lightshade swayed. The painting on the wall looked familiar. I wondered where I'd seen it before. Then I knew.

'Billy?'

'What happened you? What were you doing above at the Treaty Stone?'

'Above at the Treaty Stone?'

'Yeah! And a crowd of people around you. You fainted, you know?'

'Did I?'

'Here. Drink this. It's Bovril.'

'Bovril?' I could have cried.

I was lying on the couch in the room I'd been sitting in two weeks before. He sat in the chair opposite, staring at me as I sipped. I sipped, staring at nothing. But there was nothing in that room except him. I could hear his breathing, a steady puff, and the twitching of his body, the drumming of his fingers, the shifting of a foot.

'What were you doing up there?' His voice was flat and a little unsteady.

'I've a cold.' I sipped.

'Elizabeth, d'you know you never give a straight answer?' He leaned forward, hands dangling between his knees. I sipped again.

'It's Wednesday evening, isn't it?' He said nothing. My next sip was a slurp. 'Gee! I sound like a pig, don't I?' He said nothing, nothing at all.

It was all a battle for the beauty and the bargains, between the pretty and the plain, the fat and the lean. Tight-lipped and brutal-looking, we sorted through skirts and blouses, trying to see ourselves in them through his eyes, aware of bosom and buttock, knee and neck, unaware of each other. I found myself relinquishing my position at a blouse rail, scented arms shooting past me, as though through me, more determined to have than me, I suppose, more knowledge-able, too, about beauty and bargains. I chose what was being chosen: I bought the uniform. But it was wrong, all wrong.

The skirt. Black. Tight. Short. I felt foolish, but looked different. Very different. I bought it without trying it on. In the privacy of the bedsit I examined it and myself. I had no tights, no blouse, no shoes. I looked girlish, sporty with my pale legs in ankle socks, sweat-shirt and black mini. Next came the shoes. High-heel. Awful. Black. Then tights that looked as though they'd never fit. The blouse was blue, a v-neck without a collar. Short sleeves. Chilly. Pearl buttons. The coat was necessary. A fun-fur, three-quarter-length, smock-like, a single oversize button at the neck. The reflection in my bedsit window didn't look convincing, yet all the parts looked right; the legs in the tights and the shoes looked right, the knees below the skirt, the waist looked right, as did the body beneath the blouse, yet it all seemed to be wrong. I tied back my hair and stared and stared, I let it hang loose and stared and stared, I loosened it again, brushing it vigorously, allowing it hang as it would.

Tears stung my eyes, but I didn't cry.
'Yes! All off and curled.'
'A body-wave?'
'I want it curly.'
'A body-wave so.'

The reflection in the bedsit window was then right, because the reflection in the bedsit window was no longer mine. It felt like freedom to see it: freedom and death.

Wednesday night came and went; I stayed in my room. I ate a little. I read a little. I dreamed a little. And reflected in my window, I could see hanging from the bedsit door the outfit, stiff-looking, like a soldier.

It was ten o'clock. Time to go. I did so. It was Wednesday night. Slowly, unsteadily I picked my way down the stairs. Slowly, unsteadily I picked my way down the street. I wasn't self-conscious. I was a woman – any woman; this is how it's supposed to be, I knew. I could stop anyone, grouped or alone, and say: 'Love, d'you have the right time on you, by any chance?' They would answer. They would notice the overly-red lips, the perfume, perhaps pity my struggle in the high-heeled shoes: but they wouldn't pity me. They'd know I knew where I was going, and why. No one would say: 'Are you okay there, Miss?' just because I stopped to admire the rushing river. No. No, they'd know I was waiting for someone, or taking a rest on my way to someone, or some grand party.

I was there in no time. Over the bridge I hobbled and scraped, past the house with the maroon-coloured door: I didn't even look at it, didn't have to, didn't need to.

There was no stopping to readjust clothing or to summon courage on reaching the door of The Treaty Bar. No. No second thoughts. No other thoughts.

His mouth was strange, lips split like a ventriloquist's dummy. It was not a smile. No. It was not that. He hadn't noticed the legs, the fun-fur, the hair. No. His eyes focused on my face alone, on what he knew, had known, I presume. I braved the silence, learning about my power. Some man said: 'Will y'go on there, Bill, and offer the lady a drink.' Another said: 'She'll think none of us knows our manners.'

'The usual?'

The others smiled and shuffled.

'O! Jaysus, Bill, you're the dark one – "The usual!" – is it? Where's he been hiding you, love?'

'C'mon, lads. Two's company ... and all the rest.'

'Aren't you going to introduce us at all, what?'

'This is Elizabeth Wallace.' He nodded at me. 'This is Joe, Dan and that's Tony.' He nodded at each of them.

I smiled. They shook my hand, holding it gently, all a little moist, then moved away, nudging Bill as they passed. One of them offered me his stool on leaving.

'Take the weight there off you feet, love.' I did.

I noticed him noticing my knees as I crossed my legs. I sipped my drink. He toyed with his. He looked as though he was about to say something, but didn't say anything. I undid the button on the fun-fur. He took a long swallow from his drink. Eventually he spoke.

'I can't believe this.' He wasn't looking at me. He was staring at the array of bottles on the wall behind the bar: staring at nothing. I sipped my drink. He toyed with his. Both of us surveyed the place, I seeing all the people behind him, and he seeing all the people behind me. Then he looked at me, long and hard, head to toe. Thinking. Waiting. I said nothing. The moments passed. Tense moments. Occasionally we held each other's gaze, each ignorant of the world within the other.

'Let me get you another drink, Elizabeth.' His tone was thick, sweet-thick, thought just bubbling under it. I knew what we looked like, sitting at that bar, silent, so aware of each other, tense. I'd seen many couples like that, their tenseness and silence an embarrassment to others, to me. His watching of me would be an embarrassment to others, I knew: I enjoyed it. Tense couples seldom speak; they touch. No. They rub. No. They caress each other. Always gone before closing time, leaving the ignorant and the married behind.

'Are you ready?'

I placed my half-empty glass beside his half-empty glass, uncrossed my legs, buttoned the button on the fun-fur. We left, his friends calling out exaggerated farewells.

We walked in silence to the house with the maroon-coloured door, I scraping along two steps behind him. It was the shoes, the damn things. I called after him.

'It's a nice night, isn't it?'

'Yeah!' He kept walking.

He said: 'Sh.' I said nothing. Nothing at all. He was running his hand up between my legs. We were sitting on the couch on which I'd been lying three weeks before, drinking Bovril. We'd been kissing. It started as soon as we came in the door; no tea, no talk. I'd put my tongue in his mouth. He put his in mine. He caught my right hand and placed it on his horn. He said: 'Squeeze. Gently.' I did. The blouse was open, my bra up around my neck. He sucked both breasts, licked, kissed, nipped, kneaded. I said nothing. Nothing at all.

He says: 'Sh, it's all right, Betty. Be quiet. I won't hurt you.'

I am naked, standing on the mat before the glow of the fire from the range. The light is off. I am five. I count my toes, bare on the mat.

'Sh, Betty.' His hand is between my legs. Course. Cold.

'Sh! Sh! Sh! Spread 'em.'

I am standing between my father's knees. He is sitting, stooped forward, his ear in my face. It is hairy and smelly. I place a foot on either side of a large red rose on the mat.

'Sh! Don't make a noise.'

He sucks air between his teeth. I squirm on his finger, the finger he has just sucked.

'Sh! Sh! Sh, Betty. Jesus!'

I am looking at the side of his head.

'That's nice, isn't it?'

He tickles me inside with his finger. I stretch and squirm and yawn.

'Sh, lovey. Upsa-daisy.' He straddles me across his knees. Course. Cold. My hands clasp around his neck so as not to fall and hurt myself and wake up the whole house.

'Keep your head up.'

I can feel his heart galloping away inside his vest. His hands grip my hips and lift me up.

'Sh! Sh! Sh! I won't hurt you, lovey. Make no noise, Betty.'

He eases me down. His eyes are closed. It feels like something frightening. Sudden. Hot. Alive. Like a puppy, like the touch of a very young puppy before its eyes are open.

'Ugh.'

He covers my mouth with his. He sucks my lips, my nose, my tongue. My face is all wet, so it is. It is in as far as his finger has been. I know it is some part of him. It is crawling in, like a caca coming out. He bends me back farther, filling my mouth with his tongue, lifting me up and down with a jerk of his knees and the pull of his hands.

Then it starts. Then it is over.

I said, I screamed: 'You fuckin' lousy bastard, you!' I had

him by the hair of the head. He was dazed, like one awakening. I staggered to my feet, like one awakening. He zipped up his pants, remaining seated, silent. I stood before him, above him, raging. I thought: I could reach now for that poker and strike him. I could. I could spring forward and scratch out his eyes. Gnaw at his face. I could. I should. I can't. I know I can't. I know I never will. I know of power, and it is his.

Three years later he was dead. My sister called to the factory one morning. I peeped through the door, checking to see who was there for me. I was surprised by her, by the growth in her. I could see everyone in her face: me, the mother, our father. We were never close: none of us were. There hadn't been enough ease for closeness. She said: 'Betty, our father's sick. He's in hospital. They don't expect him to last the week.'

'Has he asked for me?'

'No.'

'You've grown so tall.'

'Betty ...' I stopped her. I shook my head and stopped her. I said: 'Philomena, did you ever straddle him?' She reddened. Tears welled in her eyes. With a tissue she mopped them and the corners of her nose. I noticed the engagement ring on her finger. I placed my hand on it: she could forgive. I said: 'Congratulations. When?'

'Six months ago. Look, Betty ...'

'There's no point at all. I don't want to know. I don't need to know. I won't be going to the funeral.' That brought fresh tears to her eyes. For a moment I thought she was actually going to embrace me, cling to me. I wondered if she'd planned on doing that on her way to tell me the news. I took a step back from her. We'd not seen each other since I'd left home; I'd not seen any of my sisters. As I stood watching her cry her big, dutiful, daughterly tears, I wondered who was this woman. People were beginning to look.

'I must be getting back.' She searched my face for a while. I saw pity there in hers, confusion too. 'All I hope is that you can live with yourself: he wasn't the worst of them.' She left.

He died.

The graveyard is beside the church, beside the school. Both gates were always painted in the same colour, silver. We played there as kids, hide-and-go-seek, tig. During weekday funerals we trooped after the teacher, marching along in double file, in double-quick time into the graveyard, having waited until the main mourners had taken up their positions beside the deep, black, wormy hole. She'd say: 'Remember now, anyone caught skitting will be punished, mind,' her eyes roving from face to face. So solemn a little group we were, standing behind the sobbing adults. We'd sob ourselves if the deceased was related to one of the school children. We'd sob because they sobbed, looking so important and self-conscious as they stood among the adults. Through the gates we filed on these serious, sad days, but over the wall we scrambled in our rush to hide-and-go-seek among the gravestones on those happy schoolday days.

The house, my home, the place where I was a child, the house with the rose-patterned hearthrug is two miles from the church and school; a mile to the turn-off, and a mile from there: a dead-end, last cottage of eight, all on the left, facing the high, stone wall, the road tapering to a grassy path, leading to the lake, a Big House ruin beyond the wall, beyond the trees so tall. Our grandparents had lived in those cottages and worked in that Big House, grandfathers on the land, grandmothers in the house and on the land, when needed. Large, hungry families grew from those cottages, were schooled stiff and cruel, most catching the boat, those remaining being caught in the boom. Men, our fathers, who'd never seen anything but the arse of a cow, built factories then, built houses, built roads; bought cars, added extensions of bathrooms and back-kitchens to their cottages, bought televisions. Women, our mothers, who'd never seen anything other than the dirt of others, worked in factories then, worked in offices, cleaned offices, concentrating on the dirt of their own; bought three-piece-suites, coat and dress outfits, bought twin-tub washing machines. The Big House was no longer needed, becoming stranded in a new Ireland. It failed, couldn't be kept, couldn't be sold.

It was the land for which the people had waited, and waited, and watched. They knew it would come, sooner or later. And it did. The day of the auction saw the people walk up the avenue for the first time, with money in their pockets for the first time. The gateway was on the main road; the servants' entrance of old was on the dead-end road, called by all The Witch's Gate. A feared place by the children of the parents with the money in their pockets.

A man by the name of McMahon bought the land.

The house was stripped, its windows boarded. Back home they went, the owners, home across the water. Abandoned but preserved, like a toy in an attic waiting to be handed down, it stood. We, the grandchildren of those who had worked there, played there.

Many said it could be a fine place again; all it needed was money. It lost its roof because of money: the owners not wanting to pay rates. They said it was a shame, such a shame.

There was a storm, a storm I remember well. It raged for a couple of days, a change-of-season storm in September. In the morning, in the cold, roaring morning we gathered at the scene of the uprooted oak, just a few feet beyond our gate. It had pulled with it a section of the high stone wall, a rubble of rock heaped in the breech; it was the only breech in the wall. Everyone said it was a shame when it wasn't rebuilt, when the barbed-wire fence was put there instead.

I remember remembering the moss spine on that dead-end road; spectacular, not in itself, but in its sudden disappearance. It is part of my first day at school memory. I was four and frightened. I dragged my heels through the summer-parched moss, copper and lime in colour, tufts of it lifting easily. Suddenly it was lush and green and spongy, holding imprints of footprints, like mud or wet sand; then treacherous, becoming soggy and slippery, to be avoided; firm and crunchy on mornings of ice, white like snow, safe like snow, an Indian-file group trooping along the ice-whitened moss. It had been an unbroken line in those days, those early school days. The first gap appeared outside Lawless's house when they got a car. It was always referred to as 'the car'.

'Was "the car" there and you passing?'

'Were they at mass in "the car"?'

'Who was in "the car"?'

'I saw "the car" in town.'

'There they go in "the car".'

'They're building a shed for "the car".'

'There they go, going down to the lake for to wash "the car".'

'They're gone to the seaside in "the car".'

'Isn't it well for them having "the car"?'

They drove neighbours to visit relatives in hospital. They drove neighbours to funerals. The moss spine disappeared at their gateway, rolled out of existence by the car. Other cars came. Within a while we all had one. Anglia. Morris Minor. Volkswagen. Other people came then, with cars like ours. Townies, my father called them. They came to the lake, usually on Sunday, bright and noisy: they swam, screeching and bawling; they played with bright balls, laughing and calling to each other; they picnicked, listening to radios; they sunbathed, half-naked and oily; they strolled, meandering lazily; we watched, hidden and envious, scoffing.

The taxi driver is strolling and smoking, looking in every direction bar mine. I hear the crunch-crunch of his footfall on the gravel. It is time to leave, I know. The grave looks wonderful, still splendid with wreaths. There is a DAD one, plastic flowers in a plastic case. Phony. The human-humped earth is still loose, almost powdery. I test it with my foot. Yes! The print remains. The taxi driver is now at the wall, looking in, but not looking at me, surveying the place, perhaps remembering his own dead. I am sure he is sad for the woman he sees alone at the fresh grave. I wonder if he is wondering how he'll make conversation with me during the five-mile journey back to the town; I wonder if he fears tears.

I have a bottle in my coat pocket, brown glass with a white tin cap. It once held vitamin tablets. It now holds urine. Mine. In the bathroom last night I held it between my legs and pissed. It filled. I capped it and washed it, then placed it in my pocket. I know he is looking, his attention caught by my movements. He can see the little brown bottle. He can guess what is to happen next. I sprinkle the liquid upon the grave, the first splash falling on the DAD case of plastic flowers. The taxi driver turns from the scene, such a private scene. I drop the bottle on the human-humped earth, heeling it to its grave.

I saw it on the way there. It amused me. Cul-de-sac. On the way back I sought it out long before reaching it, eyes lingering, head turning, intrigued by it. An upright rectangle, like a hand commanding STOP. Cul-de-sac. The words on white, in black. I knew what it meant, I knew it meant dead-end. I looked it up in a dictionary in Easons. French for 'sack bottom'. That's what it means, that's what it really means. It rankled. I would laugh, scoff. I'd say cul-de-sac, then I'd scoff. I wasn't angry, but it felt like that. Cul-de-fucking-sac. Ha! I'd put it from my mind. But it rankled, like an insult, like being short-changed, not being invited, not being quick-tongued to quick-tongued barbs, being left with much to say but no one to hear it, left with much to feel without understanding the feeling. Without words. Hurt. I searched for my dissatisfaction, searched for a name for it. Cul-de-sac. That's all I could say. I'd say it after day-dreaming for hours at my bedsit window, or when I'd awake, lying there before rising. Then it was whispered, mixed with a sigh. Sad, almost. Once, I used it in a lie.

It was in the launderette late one Saturday evening. It was obviously her first time there. I helped her, showed her where everything was, advised her on the amount of powder and temperature and cycle, told her which washer was best. She was young, younger than I. She said: 'I've been in Limerick only two weeks. It's not a bad place at all.' That was how the conversation started. She continued, telling me about her job as a legal secretary. She was lonely and young, so she told a lot. One of her bosses fancied her too – she could tell by the way he looked at her. I smiled. She told about the flat she shared with three others.

'Squares, the lot of them. One is my first cousin. Mother's decision – wouldn't you know.'

'Mother' without 'my' made her sound posh. I smiled. Mother agreed she need not come home every weekend, once a month would be all right. Thurles was home. And her sister! That was why she chose to do her laundry in Limerick.

'Every stitch I have she takes, without so much as a by your leave.'

It was Father she missed most.

'Fathers can be soft on daughters.'

I smiled. She was beginning to bore me. I'd stopped listening. Her voice droned on.

'And you?'

'He's dead.' She said nothing, just stood staring at me as though slapped across the face.

'I'm sorry, I didn't mean to pry. I only wondered ...' She tailed off. I saw my mistake. 'I'm sorry. You mean do I live in a flat?'

She nodded, but I could see she'd have grasped at

anything in order to get us both off the hook.

'Yes. A bedsit in William Street. The room is big, the rent cheap. It is so convenient to work and shops, not to mention discos and pubs.'

She'd turned from me, her eyes focused on the swirling clothes. She was very young-looking.

'I found sharing such a bore – you know what I mean?' It was a question. She didn't answer.

'Home's five miles away. One has to leave sometime. You've no independence once you've your feet under someone else's table.'

I paused. Her laundry was spinning violently, loudly. 'It was hard to leave. It was ... is a lovely place. A cul-de-sac. Very private. By a lake. The same families have lived there for generations.' My voice was loud: the spinning had stopped.

She was loading the drier. She had not spoken. I was tempted to ask her if she'd heard a word I'd been saying. 'I spend a week there at Christmas and one or two weekends throughout the year.' I paused, waiting for some sort of reaction from her. 'Mother finds it lonely without Dad.' I smiled. 'We keep telling her she should get herself a companion. But you know how elderly people are when it comes to practical thinking!' I felt like laughing and crying and screaming.

'You've not been listening to a fucking word I've been saying – have you?' I said it calmly, in a low voice. She took a step back, half smiling, gasping for words. We stared at each other.

'I beg your pardon, but I've heard every word you've been saying. You've been telling me all about yourself and your family in the country.' We continued to stare at each other. She looked sorry. Sorry for herself or sorry for me, I could not tell.

'I know. Elderly people can be difficult to cope with.' Her tone was challenging, level, like one offering evidence.

I sneered. Tears welled; blinding me. I chuckled. I moved back from her, hugging my refuse sack of laundry. I opened the door, and standing there, I said: 'You know sweet fuck-all. Sweet fuck-all. D'you hear me? I've not been home since I was your age. And no one's come looking for me either.' Those words felt strange, like waking to the sound of your own voice while dreaming, and trying to remember why you're saying what you've heard yourself say. I continued, calmer, almost conversationally.

'I was there this week for the first time. And do you know why?'

Other faces were looking at me, while more were pretending not to notice. I said nothing. Blood buzzed in my ears, pounding through my head, wave after wave, pulsing. I said: 'No.' It was a whimper. I backed away from the place, clutching my black bag of rags. Up the street I tripped, fighting the urge to scream, fighting the urge to simply fall down, collapse, belly-up before them all. I could see it, the concern on the faces that would try to get me to talk, some bold leader – a man, no doubt – telling another to phone for an ambulance, my head being propped with someone's jacket, warm with the warmth of body heat. And then I would lie in a white bed, not alone. I said: 'No.' It was a groan not a word. I was at the street door to the bedsit. I stood before it, refuse sack clutched to me, like a child, like the first day, the last day of home.

I was prepared for smallness. Books about going back tell you that, tell you how the places of childhood – rooms, trees, rivers, walls – become small, dwarfed by life, time. I say: 'Next turn right, the cul-de-sac.' The taxi driver yes-nods. He says: 'Nice place this.' I take a deep, deep breath, quivering, like a body about to plunge to the depths. And like a child in a fairground, my eyes, mind, my head darts, races and twists, my body rigid, trying to take in everything. Left. Right. Ahead. Back. Up. Down.

'Say when.'

'Keep going.' Down. Up. Back. Ahead. Right. Left. The lake.

'I guess this is the end of the line, lady.' A television accent, covering concern, his eyes betraying him as he nervously looks around. I cannot speak. To the clunk of the car door closing, a duck-flock rises up, up, then veers back, instinctively cautious, but greedy for tit-bits. Left. Right. Ahead. Back again. I scan the lake, unable to think. I see, but don't. I am deafened. I am crowded. I am alone. I feel it. I know it. I can say it. I say: 'I am alone.'

Calmly I stoop to the lapping lake-water, churning it with my hand. I say: 'Blameless water,' watching it drip from my fingers. I turn. The driver is waiting in his taxi, watching but not watching. I look beyond him to the road, to the houses flanking the road, on both sides now. I stroll towards him. He looks away. I say: 'I'll meet you at the junction, okay?'

'You're the boss, lady. But don't forget, the meter's running.'

I nod and smile.

I walked that mile, through an aisle of something old, something new: memory and the present. The elms were gone, missing, like teeth. The oaks, the ash, the beeches still stood, tall and proud and eternal, making the new roofs behind and about them look wrong, all arches and angles intruding through them; past the wall, patches of colours, glaring, garish, like a prostitute seen weaving through a crowd. Big houses for people with good jobs. And the cottages, like your old aunt at a wedding: gay and confident and strange in a style new to her. They had trees of their own, the cottages; racing poplars, the height of an oak without the age or the body. And willows that wept, streaming over walls of stone, small walls of stone where privet hedges once were. Something older, something newer, the two types of cottage then; the newer belonging to those who grew up there and stayed, the older type belonging to those who came. Those who stayed: educated, an asset to the multi-national that employed them, more confident than God-fearing, families planned by wives who worked, people with a lot of pride and a little shame, shame of fathers who laboured, mothers of ten, and pissing behind bushes. It was these who inherited cottages with badly built, self-conscious-looking extensions – the toilet as much an out-house as ever. It was they who had the confidence, the shame, the pride to create something new from something old, their cottages became longer, became deeper, became like bungalows, complete and confident, like a man in a new suit.

Those who came were townies; educated, an asset to the multi-national that employed them, children of parents who once worked the land, parents who suddenly found themselves in a better world. Some who came were flower-power types, determined to be free of urban living, have a goat, keep hens and free range children. The cottages were bargains to them, near church and school and lake and only ten minutes in the car from the shopping centre on the outskirts of town. Old-world window frames painted yellow, three-legged black pots displaying geraniums, blood-red rambling roses drooping over white picket fences, names like Rose Cottage and Oak Lodge: this was old become new-old, like a suit turned, or midnight. We met along the way. Strangers. Friendly but distant, like guests at a wedding.

I'd sat in a legal office one day and signed away my share of our house. A will hadn't been made. The sisters sold it. An artist bought it. 'Art Gallery' said a sign, white on black. The house had been completely altered, looking less like a cottage than the rest, and not at all like the bungalow-types. Alpine and airy is how it looked. Yellow shutters with heart-holes in their centres flanked the windows. The roof had been raised, steep, like a church. And at the gable end, the one facing the lake, just under the roof, a pair of French windows opened onto a wooden veranda, which was propped from beneath by two stout, round, wooden poles. The roof overhung this veranda. And from its wooden railing hung a hedge of geraniums, all reds, pinks, purples, mauves, whites, smothering a background of green.

At the junction the taxi driver waited, searching anxiously for his fare's return. He held the door open for me: courtesy, or a mark of my oddness. He said: 'Want to go home now?'

'Yes. I do.'

That evening in the supermarket I bought a geranium, a pink one in a pot, which I placed on my window with a saucer beneath it, like at home. And looking at it, in that summer, dusk-dimmed room, I knew all that was left of home was in my head, like roots in clay. Nothing familiar remained.

One. Two. Three. They stood inside on the kitchen windowsill, pots of pink geraniums, rich-green, rich-pink, nourished sentries reaching beyond the net curtains which hung from halfway down the window. The table beneath, busy, bare, busy, bare. Milk in a jug, salt in an egg cup, sugar in a bowl dotted with nuggets of golden tea-splashes, butter with its wrapper tuck-balled about it, all stood in the centre of the table, the oilcloth pattern fresh and unworn beneath them, becoming faded and bleached towards the edges. By dusk, the curtains drawn, geranium pots placed on the table. Dying flower heads snapped off and discarded, off-shoot growth pinched out, used tea leaves considered a tonic, pots tapped to gauge moistness, standing in a basin soaking their fill, sitting on the outside sill, looking luscious and exotic in balmy, summertime drizzle, slips in a jam jar of water, the next generation: so she cared for them. Behind them she sat for her lifetime, seeing, hiding. In that silence back then, all I could see was a woman by a window. My mother.

A petal falls: an event in my quiet, dusk-filled room. A swaying glide down by a pink, heart-shaped petal. I wait, watching to see if others will follow. No, none. I am sitting on a chair facing my geranium. The petal settles. I shudder, not cold, not weary, but ready. The tears well up. Simple tears, no sobbing or heaving or contortions of the mouth or face. Simple, streaming tears. The moistened cheek-flesh tightens. From behind the tears the world is distorted. Huge. Wavering. The plant before me now hers, my plant multiplied by my tears, then mine again as the tears flow, the lens briefly broken. The street lights come on, shutting out the dusk, bringing darkness. My face, the face in the window, clear and distinct before fresh tears well, then it is hers. So sad a face. I go to the mirror on the wardrobe door. My face is red-blotched and sticky-looking, skin tight, lips puffed. More tears flow. I say: 'My mother ... ' I try again. I say: I tell myself: 'My mother killed herself.'

Her geraniums died when she died. I remember them: rigid, brown-stemmed skeletons.

I've not been to her grave because her grave's in Kerry: suicide corpse in sacred ground. Her family came to take their dead daughter home, crying tears of bewilderment, shame, anger, sorrow. They said: 'O! What an accident, what an awful accident. God'll be good to her.' So they took their daughter, who had died in the fire, home, her coffin shouldered by the man who had walked her down the aisle.

'Here comes the bride. Here comes the bride.'

The bride came. A life among strangers on a dead-end road came. Children came. Joy for a while, then sourness came. Confusion and doubt came, followed by apathy. Last came anger, real anger, silent, desperate, final, lonely: her motherhood, my childhood.

Hand in hand we walked that road, my mother, my sister, myself; in ribbons and bows we skipped along to her stride, to mass, to school, to the lake. She became sad and tired, then fat and tired, so my sister and I walked alone. Mary was born. She wept a lot, slept a lot, while we looked after the baby, our father, the place, her, ourselves: a giggling duo playing house. I was five, Philomena four. She gave us our orders from the bedroom, or from a chair by the fire in the kitchen. She'd say: 'Betty, put on the spuds there for the dinner, will you, like a good girl.' We'd be absorbed in something childish, say, like colouring or reading or simply examining the pictures in our library books. I'd say: 'Are you coming?' And Philomena would follow me to the pit at the back of the house. We'd make a game, naturally, probing through the huge belly of a sleeping demon for the treasure hidden within. And washing them too was a game, looking for funny shapes or spuds with faces or 'I can do them faster than you can!' She'd say: 'Big ones on the bottom, small ones on the top.'

I wrinkle my forehead and puff a sigh, disappointed in myself for not having remembered – again. So I empty the pot and line them all up: 'One, two: buckle my shoe. Three, four: knock at the door ... ' a golden necklace – the demon's own treasure – to be ordered by size.

And even from the bedroom she'd know our mistakes, like God on the wall; our lives guarded, protected, ruled by that picture of the Sacred Heart of Jesus – feminine hands with bleeding slits – which glared down on the world. God to us children, since God has an all-seeing eye: 'God's watching you, mind.' And he was, from that picture, because no matter where I stood in the kitchen those eyes were looking directly at me. She'd say: 'Big ones on the top, small ones on the bottom.'

She'd say: 'Did you remember to sweep under the table?' We hadn't.

She'd say: 'Did you close the damper on the range?' We hadn't.

She'd say: 'Did you put a drop of Dettol in the piss-pots?' We hadn't.

She'd say: 'Did you remember to feed the hens?' We had.

She'd say: 'Did you remember to bring in the eggs?' We hadn't.

Ten-to-five, that's when she got up from her snooze. I'd stand at the bedroom door and say: 'Mama, the small hand is at five, the big one is at ten. You said to call you.' She'd grown out of the bed, yawning, straightening her clothes about her as her feet nudged into their slippers. In the kitchen she'd reach for the hairbrush on the shelf above the range, clawing from it a knot of hairs, tossing them into the fire – a hiss and a quick flash, hair melting to smoke, then one, two pulls of the brush on the right side of her head, one, two pulls of the brush on the left, one, two pulls of the brush down the back of her head. No mirror. Nothing at all. She'd say: 'Those spuds are ready for straining:' his bicycle clattering against the wall.

She bustled then from table to range to dresser to table again, billows of steam from the pots pressing down from the ceiling. She'd splash limp leaves of cabbage onto a dish, her mouth whistle-blowing the steam from her face as she chop, chop, chopped the cabbage, spinning the dish a half-turn, then chop, chop, chop again, causing the limp leaves to develop into a mound of little square cells, a forkful snapped into her mouth before sweeping from the dish portions of the celled cabbage onto each bare plate, one for daddy bear, one for Betty bear, one for Philomena bear.

And then the meat: portion of pig forked from the pot, pink flesh, pearl fat, buff skin, stubbled skin, shivering and steaming, spluttering and spitting when pierced by the fork, calmer when cooler, slice gathering upon slice like biscuits shuffled from their packet. From a slice, usually the first, she cut a small piece and popped it in her mouth, gobbling it back, five or six more slices sliced before her verdict: ''Tis done.' Lips licked.

The slices sliced last were thicker than those sliced first:

his and ours. Dangling from one prong of her fork, like bait from a hook, my slice would land on my plate like a letter on a mat. He'd have his spuds peeled by then, expertly stripped by adult hands. I'd struggle with mine; it was poised on the fork, threatening to split and fall apart under the clumsiness of my childhood knife-hand, and when it did fall apart, I'd place the pieces on the plate, whittling away at the fragments pinned in position by my fork. Into my tongue-tip-held-between-teeth concentration would roll a steaming, peeled potato. I'd continue with my task, and within seconds another rolls onto my plate, both then fork-chopped in half, then fork-mashed, a fall of salt raining from her other hand, then potato and cabbage folded together.

'Leave none of that behind you now, mind.'

She'd be chewing a mouthful of my mashed cabbage and spud while scooping out the milk well in the mash-mound, a splash of milk from my cup spilt in there, then mash, mash, mashed again. Before moving to Philomena's plate, she'd slice my bacon into bite-sized pieces, popping one in her mouth like a sweet.

Philomena isn't really grown up at all because she has to have her bacon mashed up with the spuds and cabbage and has to eat her dinner with a spoon. I eat mine with a fork and I have a knife too, so I do.

Then she'd splash more limp leaves onto the dish, chop, chop, chopping: he was ready for more. And spuds were needed too, so she shuffled to the range and back again, then over to the press, filling the milk jug, then back to the range settling the kettle for the tea. Then she'd notice that Philomena was poking her cabbage out from the mashed spud, so she'd swoop upon the plate, spinning it while she mash, mash, mashed, folding in the conspicuous lump of green gathering on the edge of the plate. She'd say: 'There's a good girl, go on now and eat up all that,' popping a forkful in her mouth – 'Yum! Yum! There'll be biscuits later on if you finish it all up.' Philomena would sit there, tap, tap, tapping the mash-mound with the back of her spoon, smoothing out the ridges left by the fork: a child bored with food, knowing that if she delays long enough, the horrible spud and cabbage will be taken from her and she'll have biscuits anyway.

He'd eat in silence but not silently: munching, chopping, forking, snorting, lips smacking, puffing, belching, sucking, sipping, his knife with a dab of salt at its tip being danced upon the back of his fork, the salt raining through the prongs, the crockery-thump of his milk cup, his breathing through his nose as he drinks, the steel scrape of knife and fork coming to rest with the knife's blade gloved in the fork's prongs, a shape on his plate like an upside down V: he was finished and it was time for biscuits and tea.

He'd tower to the armchair by the fire, unbuttoning a button or two on his trousers, newspaper hauled from inside his jacket – a sports jacket once a good jacket, now a work jacket: frayed cuffs, odd buttons, a shiny, stiff, black, dirt-encrusted collar and a work smell. Slowly he'd unfold the paper, fold stretching to fold until he disappeared behind it.

She'd trot with the pot to the front door, flushed now and still gobbling down a mouthful of something, she'd toss the used tealeaves onto the gravel beyond the step. Tea leaves fist-measure into the warmed pot, followed by the bubbling, boiling water. Five minutes to draw, during which she gets cups from the dresser, more milk for the jug, biscuits from a tin box in a high hiding place, spoons from a drawer, then back to the range for the pot. Golden flow from spout to cup, like a translucent stem, flecks of tea leaf trapped there, the flow becoming darker on reaching the last cup: his cup filling. Plonk! Plinkity! Plink: milk splash-dripping, the tea now cooled and darkened, then spoon-swirled and sugar-sweetened, handed to him where he sat. Ginger Nut. Goldgrain. Marietta. Polo: all the usual. Mikado. Coconut

Creams. Kimberley. Butter Creams. Milkchoc Goldgrain: all for the special occasions – communion day, confirmation, christening, Christmas, Easter and the odd Sunday when visited by the odd aunt or uncle.

He ate none. Never. He'd slurp his tea, smack his lips on swallowing it, emitting a satisfied: 'Ahh! That's the stuff.'

That Philomena is really a silly little baby because she dunks the Marietta biscuit in her tea and it's too soft and she leaves it in the tea for too long anyway and the piece in there falls off and into her cup and she has to spoon it out and she sucks it off the spoon.

'You're only supposed to dunk the Ginger Nut, you know. You're stupid.'

'I'm not stupid.'

'You are so, stupid.'

Only then would she sit. Onto his chair she would flop, taking up his knife and fork and peeling for herself a potato or two, slicing some meat and chopping some cabbage, all onto his plate.

And there we'd be – one, happy family: a woman called 'Mama' eating her dinner from the plate used by a man called 'Dada', who sat by the fire, served and satisfied, two children: all-seeing, but dumb. Three worlds in one.

Later, she sits by the fire – dishes washed and put away, cats given the scraps, tomorrow's bacon steeping in a bowl, geraniums on the table, curtains drawn, school books on the table, light switched on, his paper read and left in some convenient place for lighting the fire in the morning. It is she who starts to speak, questions and queries about his day.

I'm not listening. I am just there.

'... Naw!'

'He's been out this good while?'

'He has.'

'Any word on the ... ?'

'Naw!'

'I suppose one of these days now that'll all change.'

'I suppose so.'

'... you'd imagine?'

'You would.'

'Something like that doesn't make sense, sure it doesn't?'

'It doesn't.'

'And do you think Flynn will get it?'

'I don't know. Maybe!'

They were the good times. But there was another time, another period before then, a time of movement and noise: joy, I suppose.

The huge red spots on her white dress are shining behind my closed eyelids. I trap the lashes with my fingers, pressing them to my cheeks while wrinkling up my forehead, tugging at the lids, stretching them: the spots remain. A burst of brightness and blindness and dancing spots dazzling me on snapping my eyes open. She is stretched on a blanket, we are by the lake, a bee buzzing around the lemonade bottle. I place my index finger on a spot to stop it from dancing. It stops. I place my thumb on another. That's too close! I stretch my thumb, the flesh between it and my finger fanning out, the skin there almost transparent; I reach another, then another with my long finger, and another with the finger next to that, and then 'this little piggy' gets a dot of its own. They are red balloons! I press them, feeling the heat of her leg's flesh. Her fingers crawl to mine.

'Betty?'

Our eyes meet. She smiles, then drops her head back on the blanket. I catch the dress' hem. One. Two. Three. Four. A noise. I look up and he is standing there, fingers splitting his pressed lips, a sign for silence, a shape like a cross. He removes that finger and points to his closed fist, shoulders hunched to his ears, face smiling, then he points down at her. I catch a glimpse of the frog in his hand, my top teeth grabbing in my bottom lip, both hands smacking onto my cheeks. Smack! Her eyes snap open.

'Who's there? What's that? Joseph? Joseph? Is that you Joe? What's that in your hand? Don't! Don't you dare, mind. I'm warning you now, mind, don't you dare ... Joseph!' She is up and running, balloons wriggling around her body, screeching, legs flying.

''Sonly a little froggie.' The white of his shirt is brilliant in the sun. I giggle with delight-fright, rolling myself up in the body-warmed, sun-warmed blanket, the sky ringing.

He is removing something from her eye.

'Joe! Not in front of the children.'

She laughs. He groans.

Mary crawled, then toddled and wobbled, and walked. Philomena and I took her out on the road, up to the cross, down to the lake, into the neighbours, swinging her between us like a straw shopping basket being hauled happily along between two kids strolling home from the shop.

'Be back in time to do the spuds.'

'Yes. We will.' And, yes, we were.

And then it ended.

It ended with a bucket of steeping working socks, socks belonging to him. She said: 'Give it a miss for one day.' She meant childhood.

'They've been there for a week.' The socks.

'All you've to do is wash 'em in some hot, sudsy water. I've the water ready here an' all for you.' Great!

'It won't take you long.' False promise.

'There's a packet of Butter Creams in the wardrobe.' The bribe.

'Can't you let those two off on their own for one turn, can't you!' She meant for good. It was for good. It was for good and for glory.

I was seven.

Down the aisle dressed in bride white, wide-eyed with pride and panic and fear and wonder, hair in ringlets, new knickers, mouth tingling from toothpaste, Jesus dangling around my neck, Corpus Christi in my mouth. Amen. A man, later, calling for my smile: communion photo upon the shelf above the range, watching: a tense virgin with a spotless soul, using reason. I can wash our father's work-socks. I can go to confession: 'Bless me father for I have sinned.' I must fast before mass because I can toddle along for communion with the grown-ups.

She'd say: 'Do what Betty tells ye to, d'ye hear me now?'
That'll show 'em: them and their stupid game.
'I know what's in the wardrobe. La! La! La-la! La!'

We learned together to cycle on her bicycle, old Philo and I; sore and sorry episodes on the High Lizzy. Whole bodies rising and falling where adults simply sat, legs twirling. We couldn't sit on the saddle and pedal; we could, though, sit there while free-wheeling, child-bodies without power, clinging to the handlebars with our thumbs, fingers stretched to the brakes, the right lever was the brake for the back wheel, the left for the front and we were warned never, ever to use it: 'You'll capsize off it and break your neck.'
'Betty!'
'Coming.'
Holding on to the carrier, I ran behind her as she struggled to pedal, wobbling along, dizzy from speed, movement jerky and unco-ordinated.
'Don't let go! Keep pedalling! Keep pedalling!'
'I can't!'
'You can!'
'I can't! I'm going to fall!'
She'd fall, as I had, seeing it as inevitable, tumbling towards the shadow of the previous one.
'Betty!'

'Coming.'

Philomena held the carrier for me. I'd say: 'Push, but don't let go.' She ran behind, laughing, screeching with delight.

'You're cycling, Betty. Betty, you're really cycling.'

'Betty!'

'Coming.'

We cut knees and elbows, grazed chins, loosened teeth, lost teeth, bruised thighs and shoulders, blackening the calf of our right legs on the oily bicycle chain.

'Betty!'

'Coming!'

We could cycle to the oak and back, to the gate beyond that and back, the bend and back, to Lawless's and back, to the lake, to the cross and back.

'Betty!'

'Coming!'

She folds the money in the shopping list, tucks it into the purse, drops that in the straw basket which she hooks on the bike's handlebar, settling it like a vest strap on a shoulder. My head pounds, heart races, palms sweat, I know I will piss: I am going to the shop – on my own, on the High Lizzy, for the messages: today, I'll fall – I'll get lost. She says: 'Don't be long now mind.' I say: 'No.'

O! The pride, the pride and fear on that journey. The shop lies beyond the school, beyond my daily path. An adventure! Trees taller there. My 'Hello' a timid burst, blushing at strangers, shy and pride-dumb on meeting children there I knew from school.

The shopkeeper said: 'You're a Wallace, aren't you?'

'Yes,' uncurling my fist, depositing on the counter the balled-up list, coins clinking.

'You're the head off your grandmother.' She asked me my age, my class at school, what subject I liked best, was the teacher cross, the names of my sisters, their ages, how was a certain uncle getting on, would raspberry jam do instead of blackberry?

She was shoulders and a head behind the counter, ebbing and flowing as she gathered together the items on the list, lining them up before my face, her face the face of an old Snow White: lipstick-red lips – drooping; powder-white skin – wrinkled; dyed-dark hair – stiff.

The cycle home was no fun at all; the straw bag, then laden with messages, was like a body, a sleeping body – moveable, but stubborn, shifting and awkward, my right knee being rhythmically nicked on each turn of the pedals. I stopped to shift the bag, settling it more forward, but back it came in no time at all. One. Two. Three. Four. Five. Six. Seven quick thrusts down on the pedals, gaining myself the ease of sitting on the saddle for a time, freewheeling along, gradually wobbling to a dangerously slow pace. Back to the pedalling again. My knee! Ouch! Ou-u-ch!

My legs were tired by the time I reached the dead-end road. Back in familiar surroundings, I felt giddy with delight, the thrill-fear of the journey having gone.

'Bang! Bang! Bang! You're dead, Lawless.'

'That's not fair. I'm not playing any more. I shot you first – you're supposed to be dead. You're cheating.'

'I'm not cheating.'

'You are so cheating.'

'I'm not cheating. What's wrong with you is you can't take your beat.'

I struggle down on the pedals, vaguely aware of the pain being inflicted on my knee, just to get past them, to be beyond them.

They quieten. Heads cocked. All eyes on me. My breathing the only sound. I hated them. It takes ages to be past them all. Beyond them I stopped, exhausted, my legs shaking, arms too, knee stinging.

'Hands up all those who want to play cops and robbers!'

'Me! Me! Me! Me!'

I walked on, unable to concentrate on the bother of cycling, wrestling then to keep the bike in a straight line.

'Hurry on, Betty! What's keeping you?' Philomena was walking towards me, Mary swinging from her hand and that of another girl, a neighbour.

'Mama says you're to let us have the bike as soon as you're back from the shop with it, so she did.' A breeze shifted, slapping my sweat-matted hair against my hot cheeks. Philomena held the bike as I lifted the basket from it. I walked on. Not far more.

'Look, Betty. Look!'

I turn. Philomena freewheeled towards me, left hand raised nervously, steering with the right.

'Only one hand!' She laughed.

The kitchen: small and warm and dark. She is asleep. I am thirsty.

'Philomena! I'm going to fall. Help! What brake do I pull?'

Our room, like any bedroom in a cottage, was small, the bed – a double bed – surrounded on three sides by the wall, a small window just to the right of it at the foot of it, the head against the inner partition wall, the door, which opened in from the kitchen, faced a picture of the virgin hanging centrally on the wall opposite, this the outer wall along which was the bed. A wardrobe was the only other item of furniture in that room, our room. There was no spare space. Two strides from the door and you were on the bed. I slept on the outside, my little sister on the inside.

And once there was a chair with its back to the side of the bed to make sure that Philomena wouldn't fall out and I'd to make sure she stayed in the inside because I was bigger than she was.

On windy nights, when the world outside our window

was alive, I told her stories, wild stories, stories with a little dread, the wind pushing and shoving against our window. She'd whisper: 'I'm frightened, Betty.'

I'd say: 'It's okay, it's only a story. It's only the wind. There's nothing to be frightened of. Nothing at all.'

Her room was on the other side of the kitchen from ours.

'Betty!'

It was the biggest of the three bedrooms.

'Betty!'

It had a fireplace, a chest of drawers and a large wardrobe, red lino on the floor, the same as in ours and the other bedroom.

'Betty!'

On the mantelpiece stood a statue of the Blessed Virgin.

'Betty!'

A crucifix on the wall above the bed.

'Betty!'

That name, my name awakened me in the mornings in that room with my sister. My mother called it until I answered.

I'd say: 'Yeah?'

'It's time to get up. Don't have me to be calling you again now, mind.' Her face, puffed, doughy, looked down on me from the doorway. She'd say: 'And whatever you do, don't wake the baby.' Across the kitchen she'd shuffle back to bed.

The kettle steams on a chair beneath the shelf where the radio is, where our only socket is, the radio's lead unplugged and hanging black and straight as a liquorice stick. I am standing beside the chair, waiting, watching the steam from the spout, at first only waving, then suddenly thick and straight. Philomena is also standing beside the chair, teapot in hand. She says: ''Tis done.'

'No, it's not. Give it another minute or two.'

She sighs, rolling her eyes to the ceiling.

'What's wrong with you?'

'Nothing. Only the kettle's boiled, that's all.'

'No, it's not.'

'Yes, it is. '

'Just shut up will you, and wait can't you.'

She mumbles something about 'stupid', her face turned from mine. The water is now bubbling in the kettle's spout. I unplug the lead, the gurgling dies slowly.

'See! I told you 'twas boiled.'

'Hold the pot steady, can't you!'

'I'll hold it steady if you stop pushing with the kettle.'

'I'm not pushing.'

'Yes, you are, so.'

My arms ache from the effort of lifting and pouring, the muscles across my chest tremble. I rest for a moment, leaving the kettle back on the chair.

'What're you doing now?'

I don't answer.

'We'll be here all morning if you don't hurry up, y'know.'

'Aw shut up, can't you! You're always going on about something. I'd like to see how long you'd hold the kettle like that for.'

'You're stupid, so you are.'

'Stop the bickering, the two of you out there,' a bawl from the bedroom.

Silence. Philomena shoots out her stiff, red, tongue at me, grimacing. I kick her on the ankle. The tongue disappears into her open mouth.

'Ouch!'

Our eyes lock, wide and staring and shocked: the baby has yelped, will yelp even more.

'That's all your fault,' I hiss at her. The yelp becomes a wail. We tussle at the back of the door for our schoolbags and coats.

'Hurry up,' we bark at each other, 'hurry up!'

The shoe stomps on the wall above our scrummaging heads, clattering to the floor. Like dancers at the end of their dance, we turn together, facing her as she stands framed in the bedroom doorway, both of us aware of the shoe in her left hand.

'If I've told ye once, I've told ye a thousand times not to waken the baby when she's asleep. Haven't I?' Her voice is calm and steady, like a priest's from the pulpit. We nod.

'Haven't I?'

'Yes,' together. The wailing of the baby dips and then rises.

'Haven't I?'

'Yes,' louder, together.

'And do ye heed me?'

We are dumb.

'Will ye ever heed me, d'ye think?'

The shoe passes from her left hand to her right, her aiming hand, her breasts heaving. We will wait until she moves; we know that the advantage is hers. It is awful, waiting. Waiting. Like reeds in the wind, we sway together, Philomena and I, ducking the shoe. We rush to the door. Escape. Swaying back, swinging open the gate.

Up that road I walked with my bag on my back, a bag with books of wonder and numbers, God and lies; wonder at the shape of my island, tracing it from the back cover of those orange copy books, large and alone, without border or neighbour; books of numbers we sang off by heart, numbers struggled over in copy books with pages of squares, counting on fingers, mutually dependent in our struggle, copying rife, the correct mark of the teacher letting me off the hook, letting her off the hook; books about God, about sin and Hell, about Hell and sin, learning that we were sinners even before we left the womb of our mothers, and books that lied, Irish books, books in that language beaten from us in our past by the English, or someone, maybe ourselves, those books showing a world I did not recognise, a world so clean and ordered and bright, like television, *mathair* in the kitchen preparing the *bricfeasta, guna deas* on her, she is slim and smiling, watching *Dadi ag ol tae*, the table set with blue and white hooped delf, *cupani agus fochupani* and fat brown eggs sitting in the matching *ubchupani*, lives lived in rooms without God on the wall or water fonts by the door; *deirigh me ar madin, ni me mo aghaidh agus mo dha laimhe*: Oh! What a wonderful lie.

'Eli-za-beth Wallace! Are you paying attention down there?'
I bought a blue banded set of ware after she was gone, six of everything, including egg-cups, plus a milk jug, sugar bowl, teapot.

When Mary was a certain age, it was reasoned she was old enough to move out of our mother's room; it was decided that the three of us, Philomena, Mary and I, couldn't all sleep in the same bed, so it was proposed that I should move to my mother's room, Mary taking Philomena's place by the wall and Philomena taking mine, and I taking the place beside my mother. This didn't make sense, not to me. I said to her:

'Why do I have to sleep with you?'
'That's the why.'
'Why can't Philomena do so instead?'
'Because she's in with Mary.'
'Why?'
'Because I say so.'
'Why does Mary have to come into our bed anyway? Can't she stay with you?'
'Can't you stop asking questions for once, can't you?'

Amanda. That's the name of my youngest sister.
Philomena was always there. Mary arrived suddenly, like a wonderful toy at Christmas, but Amanda was expected.
The shopkeeper, with her old Snow White head, had

been asking for weeks: 'And how's your mother?' Or, with her face averted while weighing tomatoes: 'Everything okay these days with your mother?' And once, before I knew about my mother's pregnancy, she said: 'You won't feel it now.' Being on summer holidays from school, I assumed she was referring to the end of the holidays. She made one of those remarks on a day when Mrs Mulrooney was present.

Mrs Mulrooney was small, fat and fresh-faced, so fat that her face never wrinkled, not when she smiled, not when she aged, she was like a balloon, shiny and stretched. You looked at her face and imagined that her cheeks would squeak if rubbed with your finger. She waddled. She wheezed. She sweated. She had ten children at home, that was her phrase.

'I've ten children at home and they've me kilt.' 'I've ten children at home and I don't know what to give them for their tea.' 'I've ten children at home, two of them are in your class at school.' 'I've ten children at home, one this year for first communion and one for confirmation, Lord help me.' 'I've ten children at home and I'm cursed with them.' 'I've ten children at home and I'm blessed with them.'

The shopkeeper had been serving me when in waddled Mrs Mulrooney.

'O! Gee-kerst! The heat's me kilt.' She hauled her body onto the stool with an upward motion of her shoulders and elbows, sitting sideways, one foot on the ground, the other dangling.

'Take a seat there, Mrs Mulrooney, and I'll be with you in a minute.'

'No rush! No rush. God is good and the day is long.'

The shopkeeper dipped the top of her pencil on her tongue and proceeded to add the numbers she'd marked down on the brown paper bag; somewhere in my straw shopping basket was the bag with the total from the previous customer. As she fumbled for my change in the round biscuit tin, she said: 'Your mother must be finding it

95

hard these days, what with the heat and everything?'

I said: 'Yes.'

'You're Wallace, aren't you?' I looked at Mrs Mulrooney's hot, lovely face.

'Yes.'

'I've ten children at home and one of them's in your class at school. D'you know Peter Mulrooney, d'you?'

'Yes.'

'Is your mother sick, or what? I haven't seen her in ages.'

I didn't know what to say. I looked at my feet, about to answer, but the shopkeeper spoke instead.

'No! Mrs Mulrooney. No. Far from it. Mrs Wallace will be having her baby any day now. Isn't that right, Betty?'

'Go way outa that. Hah! I never knew – never heard a word. A new baby! You must be delighted?'

'Yes.' The shop felt small, hot, crowded.

'Ye've all girls in yer house, so I suppose ye'll be hoping for a boy. I've six girls in my house at home and four boys, God help me! The girls are great, though. I'd be lost without them, but it's nice to have the boys as well, isn't it? A baby! Well, now that's great news altogether – great news entirely. And isn't your mother the lucky woman to have a fine girl like you yourself. You must be ten, or thereabouts? – the same age as my Peter at home.'

'Yes. Goodbye now, I must be going.'

'O! Goodbye, goodbye. Tell your mother I was asking for her, and I might be down for a visit as soon as the baby ...'

I wheeled the High Lizzy out of the shopkeeper's yard, knees shaking. I wheeled it along the road, taking short, slow steps. It made sense. I was happy. It all made sense. Thoughts and thoughts raced through my head, filled my head, dizzied my head. Tears came before the sobbing, and when the sobbing came, I could walk no more. In the grass beside the road I sat, pretending to be removing a stone from my shoe, just in case anyone passed. So I sat.

The baby would come out of her belly, out between her

legs. It would have been in there for nine months. It had got there because they had prayed very hard to holy God. I knew those things. And I knew that that was why she had become so cross. It had to be. It had to be that. Being pregnant had to hurt, like eating too many crab apples and swelling out like that. I forced out my belly, feeling it press and strain against my clothes. See! It hurt. She didn't hate me: it was the pain. It was all that pain that made her so cross. And waiting for the pain she was going to have when the baby was coming out. It made sense. It all made sense. It would end. The baby would be born and she would not be cross any more. She would be up again – a time would come when change would come. This was new, different. This wasn't like expecting Christmas or my birthday, because nothing was really very different after them. This was exciting, but not the type of feeling where I couldn't wait for that certain time to come, it was a stronger, deeper excitement because I could wait, and knew all I had to do was wait and life would become the old life of before, in time to come, in the future. And I knew, above all I knew, she did not hate me: she did not, after all, know it was I who had put the razorblade in her shoe.

I picked a pebble from the road and rolled it between both palms, feeling it press painfully on my flesh.

It wasn't my fault, so it wasn't. It wasn't my fault. She made me do it. She drove me to it. I warned her. I told her it wasn't fair, picking on me all the time. It wasn't fair. I said: 'Why don't you get Philomena to do something for a change?' She said nothing, just stayed looking at me with her mouth open. I said: 'It isn't fair, picking on me all the time.'

She said: 'Get up off that chair and do what you're told, before I break every bone in your body.'

I rolled the pebble more tightly, my palms pain-tingling and hot.

A summer Sunday, heavy, hot. We've had the usual meal of roast chicken, roast spuds, marrowfat peas, strawberry jelly and custard; we've had the usual mass, she and I at the first, in with the old, the untidy, mothers concerned to have good dinners ready for big families, the unfashionable mass, many bicycles, few cars, no hats. The ceremony is a mystery to her, missing the Latin and the priest's back. Philomena has had her usual Sunday morning, a stroll with her friends to eleven o'clock mass, Mary held by the hand, a merry band of tittering boys and girls, whispering, coy, loud, flirting, showing off, learning something. He has had his, up late and sour, scattering females before him.

'My shoes? My shirt? My tea? My cap? My bike? You bitch!'

Last mass and alcohol.

'The bastard! Here he is, drunk again. After all I said.'

Gay and strange, he gives us our affection for the week: a packet of Colleen sweets between us.

We've had our usual Sunday dinner. Tasty. Tense. Gobbled by him, appetite edged by alcohol, gobbled by her, appetite edged by anger, gobbled by us, appetite edged by them. Then sleep for them both: the sanctuary on Sundays. He to his bed, fully clothed, on his back, on top of the blankets to snort and snore, she by the range, head in her chest, hands on her lap, breathing steadily. She had a dread of visitors calling on Sundays, so she slept by the range, having a greater fear of being caught in bed.

Philomena was doing her usual Sunday chore, keeping Mary out of the sleepers' way. They were at the lake, an amenity area by then, tar, tables and life-buoy, rubbish that spilled from overflowing bins. It was usually thronged on Sundays, with people coming in their cars from the town; Morris Minor, Austin A 40, Volkswagen and others trooped down our road from midday onwards on summer Sundays. He'd say: 'There goes the townies!' She'd say: 'Isn't it well for them!' He'd say: 'Good for nothing but backing horses and eating fish and chips!'

They brought their world with them; stylish mothers and fathers, loud radios, noisy children, children without shyness, big, bright, slow-bouncing, multi-coloured beach balls, picnics and pet dogs. We played together: children attract children. They shared their ball with us, and we took them exploring the area, especially the old ruins in the field behind the high stone wall. Their parents asked us the usual questions adults ask children.

'What's your name?'

'Where do you live?'

'Have you many brothers and sisters?'

'What age are you?'

'What school do you go to?'

'What class are you in?'

They would tell us they'd grown up in a place like ours, that their brother or sister or mother or father still lived there, that they go back every Christmas or Easter or summer for a visit, just to see the old place again.

She says: 'Can't you go on along down to the lake, can't you?'

The dishes are done, the floor is swept and the cats have had the scraps.

'The lake's stupid, so it is.'

'What's stupid about it? Can't you go and find Philomena and Mary and have a game with them, or something?'

She is settling in her chair, ready for her nap.

'I want to watch the telly.'

'No. You can't. Not on a fine day like this, you can't.'

Her head is tilted up, resting against the back of the chair. I wait. Her eyes droop. Her mouth draws open. The screen flares, then darkens, a buzz buzzing, fading as the picture comes into focus.

'I said no.'

She folds her arms.

'I'll keep it low, so I will.'

'I said no.' Her words a mumble, her chin dipping to her chest.

So, in that room on that Sunday I sat watching the television screen, images flickering silently. It didn't really matter that I couldn't hear; what mattered was that it was my choice.

Slowly her breathing deepens, her head rising and falling on her chest; his snores from the room building gradually in fits and starts, calling out: 'Wha! Wha! Wha!' – soft barks as he slips to his sleep, the bed-springs creaking to his involuntary leap. At the honk of his snore, I turn up the volume ever so carefully, ever so marginally, taking a backward glance at her to see if she's noticed. She hasn't. I continue to watch the screen, even though I still cannot hear what they are saying, a man, a woman, a young boy.

A car passes: more townies to the lake. I turn the volume way down, then press the other channel buttons, nothing from them but hiss, hum and a screen full of shimmering dots. Back to the man, the woman, the boy. They are poor, I can tell by their clothes. They live off the land in the country part of America. There are no Indians. The boy wears long pants, so he must be a big boy, past confirmation; there are no other children in the family.

The rhythm of his snoring stops, the bed creaking and groaning as he turns over. I look at her, watching as she chews in her sleep. His snoring starts again.

A bee buzzes into the kitchen, in through the open doorway. It swings slowly, fat, black, and blind by the way it keeps swinging up close to everything, then suddenly backing away, only to find itself up against something else. It keeps lunging at me. I can see its two, big, shiny eyes. Careful not to waken her, I grab the dishcloth, swinging it lightly at the bee, more in an effort at directing it towards the door than killing it. Across the kitchen we silently dance, up again, down again, to the left, to the right, to the left again, over and back, and finally out. Up into the air it goes, quickly, as though sucked, glad to be free. I hear a call like that call of the peacock, a pure, clear sound as I stand watching the bee's flight to the sun, the call comes from the lake, the cry of a child at play.

The man, the woman and the boy live in a timber house. The man wears black dungarees, the same as the boy's, the woman wearing a long black dress with a long white apron over it. A man comes by on a horse, staying on his horse as he speaks to them. He wears a black ribbon, bow-tied in his shirt collar. He has a ring on his finger. He smokes a cigar. The man and the woman stand looking after him when he leaves, their worried faces taking up the whole screen.

She is fast asleep, her feet stretched out, crossed, her right ankle resting on the left, the toes of her bare feet twitching. I turn up the volume, my eyes on her. She hears nothing. I think about the Butter Creams in her wardrobe.

'Come here, little fella,' the young boy says.

He has found a baby dear, a doe. Those eyes! The little ears! The shiny nose! It is beautiful. So beautiful. It is injured. It limps. It struggles to its feet, ready to run, but those delicate little legs fold and it sits there flicking its little tail.

'Don't be afraid, little thing. I won't harm you,' the young boy says, reaching slowly to stroke the doe's head, moving closer and closer as he speaks, until finally he is sitting right beside it. He carries the doe home in his arms, struggling and stumbling under its weight, all the while mumbling words of reassurance.

'Don't worry, it won't be long now. We'll have a look at that leg of yours, have you up and about in no time at all. My Pa's pretty good at fixing most anything, you'll see. Don't worry, not long more. And Ma, too, she's pretty good at sorting out where it hurts.'

On and on he goes, sweat breaking out on his forehead as he struggles along. Home at last. His Ma comes to meet him at the porch, drying her hands on her long apron.

'What you got there, son?'

And then she starts questioning and cooing and stroking and smiling and feeling the creature's sore leg. And they decide to wait for Pa to come in, and Pa comes in and the questions start all over again, Ma explaining the story to him. And finally they fix up the leg with pieces of stick bound over with strips of material. And in a few days the doe is up and about, hobbling around on its bound-up leg, and the young boy gets it to feed from his hand and he smiles at Ma and Ma smiles at him and the sun is shining.

That man on the horse comes again, saying something about rent and stuff like that, and there's lots of other talk about Pa working hard and Ma working hard and crops and harvest and debt and money. But the doe, the doe is getting better, the young boy spending all his spare time looking after it and helping it along.

And then something goes wrong. The doe eats some of Pa's crops. Pa is angry. The boy is upset. But Ma manages to make things all right. But the boy is still sad. He talks to the doe, telling it how grown-ups don't understand. The doe is to live in a pen and that's why the young boy isn't happy. And Pa isn't happy because the wire for the pen is going to cost so much. The pen is small. Then things get really bad because the doe jumps clear out of the pen and where does it go but straight into Pa's crops again. In the morning Pa sees the damage that's been done to his crops. It is raining. Pa gets his gun. The young boy cries and cries: 'It's all so unfair. Everyone is so cruel. Just one more chance. Please, Pa!' The boy screams at Pa, he screams and he cries, and I cry, and he screams as Pa walks off with his gun to the waiting deer.

'Betty! Can't you put on the kettle there, like a good girl, and make a cup of tea?'

'Why are you always picking on me?' I scream, tears pouring down my face. 'Why?' I scream, shaking, sobbing, suddenly frightened, fingers clasping and unclasping, bubbles bursting from my mouth and nose. She looks a little shocked. She says nothing. I feel trapped, afraid. I want to run. Bang! A gunshot? No. The smack of her shoe against the wall. It missed me.

'Get up out of that, you bitch you, and stop giving back-answers to me, d'you hear? Make the tea when you're told.'

'Pa! Don't. Please, Pa ...'

'I won't. I won't. I won't make the tea. Make it yourself.'

Blind like the bee, I stumble close to everything as I run from the house.

'Go on! Give it to her, the bitch,' his roar from the room as I pass.

A summer Sunday, and all is well. He's in his drunken, swollen sleep, she's by the range, asleep with her dread, the others are gone out to play, like good children. I know my world. On the floor I sit, beside the bed, my bed, her bed, our bed, knees up and spread, her shoes between my feet.

Eeny, meeny, miney, mo.
Catch a tiger by the toe.
If he squeals, let him go.
Eeny, meeny, miney, mo.

The left one. The left shoe gets the razorblade.

It all made sense. I threw the stone from me. It all made so much sense. I was bad, pure bad. I deserved bad things done to me.

Amanda.

She arrived home with our new baby sister, telling us that her name was to be Amanda. He said: 'Amanda?' And said no more.

Philomena and Mary liked the name; I liked it, but

wondered. It wasn't news that we'd had a baby sister: it was news that we'd a baby sister named Amanda. There was none of those usual 'who does she look like?' questions, or questions about her weight, or hair colour or was she cross, it was the name about which they were curious. Some said: 'Fair play to her.' More said: 'Amanda? Where did she get a name like that?' A few said: 'Tell your mother that Amanda is a grand name, and that I said so.'

Night feed.

New baby. Old mother. New night-dress, bought for the occasion of the delivery. I awake in the night time to flashlight and movement, her heat pulled away from me, hearing the stop-start cry of Amanda. My mother's back is to me, her shape huge in the dimness, mewling, answering the cry. From a flask she pours warm milk into Amanda's bottle, squirting a drop onto the back of her hand, checking its temperature. Satisfied, she leans forward and picks up Amanda from her cot. Silence. Sucking sounds then from Amanda, whose hands and feet wriggle like jelly as she settles to her feeding. Upright in the bed my mother sits, swaying gently, her eyes on the face of the baby in her arms, a finger darting from either hand to rub a cheek, smooth a curl, or tease a fist to grasp it.

No one called to our house in order to see the new baby; there was no need for them to do so.

Amanda was born on the first day of September. School began for everyone that week, except for me. I remained at home until the end of the month, looking after everything. Twice daily, morning and evening, I wheeled Amanda up and down that dead-end road. In the mornings I was on the road in time to meet neighbours on their way back from walking first-time schoolchildren to school, meeting even more of them in the afternoon.

It was a strange time. I loved it. I hated it. I loved her bustle again in the mornings. I loved the order her presence made. She was up with us, sometimes even before us, the kitchen warmed from her activities of washing and feeding and dressing Amanda. Tea was ready. I'd cut and wrap lunches for the two, feeling guilty, feeling useless, wanting her to see how good I was. Her face looked different, as did her eyes, like someone working out a difficult sum. Amanda, wrapped like a butcher's parcel, was finally placed in the pram, pink-faced and peaceful, a string of pastel-coloured rattling ducks within reach of her dancing hands.

She'd say: 'Now! She's ready. Take her as far as the cross and back, and be careful. Keep well in if a car comes. D'you hear me?'

After the first morning, I knew what she wanted: she wanted to show off Amanda, depriving neighbours of their chance to be in our house. I nearly died when I met some women on their way back from the school. They said: 'Amanda? Isn't she beautiful? Aren't you good. How's your mother?'

When I'd return she'd want to know whom I had met, what did they say, what did I say. She was in bed. It was the same in the afternoon. It was the same every day. I hated it.

She'd say: 'Now! She's ready,' her eyes bright, fixed on the clock. They'd say: 'Out again, Betty! Aren't you great. How's your mother? That Amanda is getting enough air anyway.' I hated them and those September days.

By October it had ended. Back to the old routine. Back to school mornings of struggle and bickering, back to days of wariness and weariness and work. Philomena and Mary got charge of Amanda, I got the nappies and the spuds and his lust.

I carry the smell of his semen to her bed. She says: 'Goodnight.'

Living was dull.

The pink planning notice appeared around that time; protected in a plastic cover, it was nailed for all to see on one of the posts supporting the barbed-wire fence which bridged the gap in the high stone wall. We could see it from our gate. He brought the news. He said: 'I suppose ye've heard?' His usual opening for startling news he'd heard in the pub, dramatic blather about sudden deaths, some farmer selling out or a frog found in someone's breakfast egg. We were neither listening nor not listening.

'McMahon's sold out. Some townie has bought the entire place right out from under him – lock, stock and barrel. And what's more, they're knocking down that old ruin and building a place twice the size of it on the very spot. Can you credit it?'

A pause. There was always that pause to gauge our reaction; usually there was none because we knew that he'd continue anyway, but that evening was different.

She looked at him, slowly turning her head in his direction. 'What're you saying now?'

'If you don't believe me, take a look for yourself.' He led us to the gate, pointing out the pink notice.

She said: 'Stay there, let ye.' The two of them went to have a closer look.

No one had bought out McMahon's land, nor was the ruin to be razed and built upon. McMahon had sold a site to someone; he'd been approached with an offer he couldn't refuse.

Our father blamed the school bus. He said: 'Now that O'Malley's put a free bus under their arses, we'll have nothing but townies coming out here to live. Wait'll you see!'

Donogh O'Malley, Jack Lynch and Fianna Fáil: I knew them well. They were giving me the chance of free education in a town school – even a free bus to take me there. He'd say: ''Tis true for the man, 'tis true for what Lynch says: "'Tis the end of serfdom for the Irish." And it's about time, too.' He'd be drunk, going on and on about it, always finishing up with the same question: 'Who'll you vote for when you grow up?'

The first fact we learned about our new neighbours was

their name: Healy. After that, all other information went through a process of modification: retired millionaire from Dublin, return of a relative of the original owners of the place, rich tinker from Galway, heirless farmer from Wicklow; the house was being built for a foreigner by a man named Healy, the foreigner a Frenchman, a German, a Dutchman.

Healy was a young solicitor from Limerick, with a wife.

The house was to be two-storey, with a basement, three-storeys – without, a bungalow with the garage underneath, there was to be a swimming pool – outdoor, indoor, a tennis court, stables, it was to be built of stone from the old ruin – brick, half stone and brick.

The house was Spanish in style, but at that time we saw it as just large and odd, with its arching windows and doorways, white walls, bright, almost-orange roof, a little house to one side of it, a miniature replica of itself, which was the garage, a paved walkway between it and the house, a portico connecting the two buildings. It was set on its side, its shoulder to us, the other to the old ruin, its front facing the setting sun and the lake. The wall for their gateway was an extension of the existing wall, both in height and material, curving back to large piers like arms closing in embrace, from which hung a set of black ornate gates.

The pink notice sat there all winter. Nothing happened. All the talk and speculation had run its course by then. The shopkeeper would ask: 'No sign of anything happening down there beside ye yet?'

Then one spring day, on our return from school, we noticed the crinkled cut running along both sides of the dead-end road. The digger had arrived. We rushed past our homes, eager to see the digger in action, our pace breaking to a run on hearing its mechanical drone. At the breach we stood, looking in, watching. Some were to stay for the rest of the evening, perched on the wall, bearing witness to the disturbance of that ancient land.

This event generated a fresh round of talk. I heard it at home, at the shop, after mass, before confessions.

'They'll never stay here in a place like this.'

'Sure what's here for them.'

'One wet winter and that'll cure 'em.'

'Too lonely for a young wife.'

'She'll never fit in.'

'No equals of their own here.'

For the next few months the building site figured in most people's day; children played there after the workers had left, delighting in nooks and crannies and the novelty of rubble, a change from playing in the old ruin; women went there to collect the children, curious about rooms that were not yet rooms, imagining another woman's things, taking with them handy pieces of timber for starting the morning's fire; then came the men, examining block-work, plastering, wood-work, exchanging tales of building sites on which they'd laboured – hard foremen and hard drinking in hard times, pocketing nails as they left; dogs came after them, nosing through lunch wrappers and milk cartons, a lick here, a crust there; then the rats, busy bodies darting along, scavenging in that world in which they were king, scattering to the footfall of my mother and me.

It was always dusk when she and I went there. She'd say: 'Betty! Get on your coat, we're going for a walk.' At first I was unsure, half-glad: it wasn't like her to suggest something which might be fun. At the building site I ran ahead, showing her this, getting her to look at that, eventually slowing my pace to hers, conscious of her indifference, strolling side by side then, a mother and an old child. She'd say: 'Run along. I'll catch up with you.' I'd walk off.

'Betty! Get on your coat, we're going for a walk.'

The house is taking shape, walls are rising, rooms closing in. I walk along hallways and enter through door-ways, even though I could step over those walls, like walking in a miniature maze. We part ways, each taking a different route. She retraces her steps, again and again. I sit to wait.

'Run along. I'll catch up with you.'

I walk off.

'Betty! Get on your coat, we're going for a walk.'

The house has a roof, but windows gape and walls are rough, like the ruin. We know where the kitchen is to be, and upstairs the bathroom suite has arrived, the pale-green bath looking funny on its four, unpainted metal feet. I turn the taps and check the toilet bowl – no water yet.

'Run along. I'll catch up with you.'

I saunter off, checking over my shoulders to see if she is coming. No. On I walk, slower and slower. No one. At the wall I wait, and wait. She comes, moving quickly. I press myself against a tree, she passes without seeing me. I wait. Then slowly I walk back to the new house, in through the doorway, looking in every room, then climbing the stairs to the next floor. A smell. The bathroom. I stand over the toilet bowl looking down on my mother's excrement.

'Betty! Get on your coat, we're going for a walk.'

The house is closed to us. It has doors, locked doors and locked windows. Round and round and round she circles the place, checking doors, checking windows. I watch.

'Run along. I'll catch up with you.' She circles the house once again.

'Do you hear me?' Crows lift from the bare spring trees at the sound of her roar.

I turn and run, running as fast as I can, running faster than I ever did before, stopping for breath at the wall, catching the sound of breaking glass.

Throughout the building period the Healys came regularly to the site; evening visits, just as the men were finishing, both of them touring the place in the company of the foreman, fingers pointing, heads nodding, heads together, poring over the plans, fingers pointing again, Sunday-best dressed, tip-toeing along through the mud of their making.

'There's no flies on them, I can tell you.'

Sometimes Saturday, sometimes Sunday they came, sometimes alone, sometimes with friends, jeans on them both, her hair in a pony-tail. Alone together they'd stroll hand in hand, or his arm across her shoulder, hers around his waist, a giggle here, bark of a laugh there.

'That'll come to an end, so it will.'

With friends they were louder: 'And here to the left ... And there to the right. Over here we plan. Later we'd like to add ...' They'd part with a volley of car horns.

'Hope it stays fine for 'em.'

One Sunday they arrived along with two children, a toddling boy, and a girl of about four or five, too like them not to be theirs. Their parenthood came as a surprise.

'A couple or more will soften their cough for 'em.'

Once the building work was finished, attention centred on the surroundings of the house. Hills of earth were swept away, creating new contours, giving a new lie to the land, tar came, grass came, trees came, shrubs in tubs stood at the doorway, lamps lined the driveway, painters scurried up and down walls for a week like giant insects, a trail of white in their wake.

'Isn't money marvellous all the same, though?'

All kinds of vans crawled uncertainly down that dead-end road, drivers doubting whether the owners of the load they were carrying lived in such a place.

'Excuse me there, love. Tell me this, is there a "Villa Rosa" anywhere around here at all?'

Cards from the ESB were delivered to us, telling us that the supply would be off for a couple of hours on a certain day. The night of that day saw the house burst into life with light, it poured from every window, the driveway like a runway when the lamps came on, the glow from them spreading as far as the trees by the high stone wall, a world protected by both, light and wall.

His car rumbles past our gate as I struggle at the breakfast.
She says: 'Is that him? Is that him?'

'Yeah. That's him.'

She dances from the bed to the window to catch a look,
questions shooting from her:

'Is he alone? What car's he driving?'

It was soon established that Mrs Healy was a solicitor as
well, leaving for work a little earlier than her husband, her
daughter beside her in the front seat of the car, school
uniform on, a beret perched on the side of her head, so sweet
and so smart in her shirt and tie. She'd dance from the bed
to the window to see them pass as well.

The short, dark-haired young one with the sallow skin,
strolling about the place with the toddler in tow was an
immediate target for strange speculation.

'Some quare goings on there, I'm telling you.'

She was French, an au pair, come to work for the Healys
for a year; a student, taking a year off in order to improve
her English: and we gave her every opportunity to do so.

'What's your name?'

'Michelle.'

'What's his name?'

'Aaron.'

'And his sister's?'

'Nena.'

'What's his age? Her age?'

'Aaron is two and Nena is five.'

'Do you like Ireland?'

'Yes.'

'Is it much like France?'

'Yes – no – a bit.'

'Are there churches there, like ours, you know?'

'Yes. A little like here.'

'I suppose Aaron's a little devil at mass?'

'A devil? I do not understand. No?'

'I mean, he's cross, like, at mass?'

'Ah! Yes, I understand. No. He is too good.'

We asked all we could dare.

'There she is! Run out and start talking to her – find out their names, can't you?'

I liked Michelle. She was something exotic. She smelt different. I loved listening to her speak, lips in a permanent pout, familiar words stretched and hardened, phrases sung in a different tune. She told me where in France she was from. After I failed to locate it on my atlas, I asked her to show me where it was; she did, delighted, telling me all about her small town, about the people there and their ways, laughing at this one, concerned about some other, critical of a few. She said: 'Betty, I've learned that people are much similar wherever you go. Even here,' she gestured towards the cottages, 'even here the people are the same as in my small town in France.' She knew the reason for all our questions.

'You all want to know about the Healys, no?' I reddened. She said: 'It is so funny because they ask me if I get to meet any of you, and what are you like.' I laughed. She laughed. She said: 'It is funny. But it is sad too that no one will talk to me about me. People are funny here.'

After that I always felt a little angry on seeing one of the neighbours 'pumping' her for information on the Healys. I knew her feelings. I knew what her place in France was like I knew her plans, and about her mother and father and sisters and brother.

Sometimes she spoke to me about things which I did not really understand, her face serious and sometimes sad. It was unfair. I didn't say no when asked to 'draw' Michelle on something concerning the Healys, but I stopped asking her those questions. She would tease me: 'Is there something you must ask, no?' At first I was offended, but later I learned to laugh with her.

Her favourite food was spaghetti bolognese. She said: 'You must come to the house one day and I will show you how to make it, no? I will tell you when to come.'

I told her Sunday afternoon was best: I'd not be missed.

I went there on a Sunday when the Healys were away for the weekend. The house was a television house, with rooms like furniture-shop window displays. She showed me through them all, all bright, all warm, all big, a blush as I was shown the bathroom; rooms like toy shops for Nena and Aaron, so many rooms in which to sit. The kitchen, big and white and cool, a room not lived in, Michelle's voice ringing slightly. There I sat, a plate of strange food before me, in one hand a fork, the other a big spoon, watching as she demonstrated the knack of twirling spaghetti onto a fork. Behind her a window, beyond which I see the trees, beyond them the wall. I think of home, sleeping home.

'Cheer up, Betty. You'll soon get the spaghetti up okay.'

Every Friday a bus passed on the main road, stopping at the cross to collect those assembled there, mostly people living on the dead-end road, but others also gathered at that point from the surrounding area, women for the most part, going to town, for the children's allowance, and pensioners collecting their pension: a day out for all. My mother made that trip every three months, that being the limit to which the children's allowance could accumulate. It was usual for me to miss school that day, minding whichever baby there was at the time.

For my mother to make a trip in between that time was very unusual. She made one of those trips when Amanda was nearly two years old, and the new house was old news. She went without a shopping bag, looking like a child going to school without a schoolbag. That evening she came through the doorway, looking as though she'd returned because she'd forgotten something and had yet to go to

113

town. Next day, Saturday, the glass-case arrived.

It arrived in the morning, and we all had to go and help the man carry it into the house; he was old, his car was old, and the glass-case was old. It was placed in a position directly opposite the front door, looking out at anyone that looked in. A kettle of water was boiled immediately, suds bubbling in the basin to the splash of boiling water. The glass-case was washed inside and out. It was tall, as tall as I was then, a half-moon shape, standing on three claw feet, with three panels of glass, having large roses printed on them at a midway point. The centre panel was fixed, the other two being doors; behind the glass were three rows of shelves. Cleaned and empty, it looked large and lost in the room. I sat watching without helping, handing cloths to her as she asked for them: a wet one, a dry one, her face rolled tightly down to her pursed lips.

He said: 'What in the name of Jaysus do you need a thing like that for, what?' I turned from him to her. She stayed looking at him until he left the kitchen. She said: 'Never marry a man.'

The box she took down from the top of the wardrobe had always been there, a brown cardboard box, not very big, and it didn't look very heavy as she carried it to the kitchen table. We were never curious about it because we never saw anything going into it or coming from it: it was just a box on top of the wardrobe, on top of which blankets and pillows were thrown. With both hands she lifted bundled bodies wrapped in yellowed newspaper from that box, laying each one gently on the table, lining them up in a row.

'I hope there's nothing broken in here, now.' She looked very important, her face half-shy, her head nodding, uttering soft sounds: 'Tch! Tch! Tch!' as each item was unwrapped, the newspaper balled-up and dropped back in the box.

The larger items were the first to be unwrapped: a pair of white dogs in sitting pose, tails curled onto their sides, a black chain curving down their bodies from their collars.

They were identical, except one sat to the left, while the other sat to the right, heads with black noses pointing out to the side. Next to unfold was a shepherd boy, crook in hand, wearing short pants of blue, a head of blond curls, his mouth open, calling, and from the bundle beside it came a little shepherdess, crook in hand, wearing a full dress of blue and a bonnet to match, around which was a cream frill, her mouth open, calling. A stopped clock, a carriage clock with Roman numerals came next; she set the correct time, winding it up tight. From an almost-round package came a teapot, little pink flowers on a cream background, a belly so big with a lid so small. I was allowed help in the unwrapping of the pieces of an eighteen-piece, china tea-set, blood-red roses on a pure white background, a golden line on the rim of the cups, saucers and side-plates. Six glasses, paper stuffed into them, came next. The last to be unwrapped was the smallest, a brass plate with a bright, city scene, under which were the words: Souvenir of Dublin.

He'd been watching her from the doorway. She said: 'Do you remember this, do you?' holding it up for him to see. He said: 'Ah! For the love and honour of Jaysus, leave me alone.'

She spent the next while placing these items in the glass-case, standing back at the door to survey each new arrangement.

They fought no more. She stopped wanting something from him; they neither loved nor hated nor even cared. He had won. There was no need but *his* need. The things he scoffed at were gone: desserts, Christmas trees, effort from her for us or him or even herself. He'd say: 'Can't you tidy yourself up, can't you?' She'd sit there, arms folded, pondering the glass-case. He'd say: 'Betty, for the love and honour of Jaysus will you ever wipe the shite from the leg of that dirty, fucking, rotten child, for Christ's sake!' – Amanda dancing in her own dung.

It has been rolling beneath the table all day, twirling to the touch of feet, Philomena and Mary play with it, rolling it to each other, having fun with an empty danno bottle. She has stopped me from throwing it out, as I am used to doing.

'Leave it there for him, the fucker. Let him throw it out.'

It twirls to the touch of his boot as he sits to the dinner I've cooked.

'Betty, is there any chance at all you'd throw out that bottle, love?' His voice sober, tone exposed.

She says: 'Betty, haven't you something better to be doing?' snapping out each word. 'Let him do it himself. Bring in some sticks for the fire for the morning, can't you, and stop hanging around there doing nothing.'

Ding! Ding! Ding! – his knife against the plate as he slices his spuds. 'Do what your father tells you, d'you hear me,' his voice more firm, anger starting.

She says: 'Bet-ty!'

Late at night upon his knee, naked, numb and wet between my legs, he is sucking my fattening breasts, breasts made fatter, pressed together, breast-flesh gripped in the clasp of his left hand. I stretch my hand up to scratch my head, breast-flesh unfurling, nipple disappearing from his mouth.

'Sit still, will you!'

I stretch and scratch again, and again.

'What's the fucking matter with you tonight?'

His lips are swollen and shiny. Shaking me, he says: 'Huh?'

'I'm itchy.'

His fingers hunt through my scalp, slowly at first, then faster and faster, then stop.

'When did you last wash that head of yours? You're crawling.'

By the time Michelle was due to leave for France, she no longer attracted much attention, nor was she sought after for the purpose of gathering information on the Healys.

For most, the Healys were no longer news. Something seemed to have been settled in people's minds when it became known that they had also purchased the land between their house and the lake. A pebbly pathway ran through this, leading to the little wooden landing pier they'd constructed at the lake. A boat-house had also been built, in a style similar to their house. They had two boats, a yellow rowing boat and a white cabin cruiser. Mr Healy seemed to be the only one ever to use the rowing boat; on fine evenings after work, or early on Saturday mornings, he'd pull out to the centre of the lake; only occasionally would the children be with him. He'd row around the small island on the lake, returning at a brisk pace, hot and heaving, he'd jog up the pathway to the house.

When the cruiser first arrived, it brought with it a succession of parties on the lake; small groups, mostly couples, noisy, brightly dressed in navy and white, came there to party on Healy's boat. The routine was usually the same: two by two they'd hop on board, screeching women calling to steady men, clinking bottles and creaking baskets having gone before them, a quick, foaming circle – maybe two – around the island, then anchor at a spot facing the house. Laughter. Music. The splash of a body in the water, calling: ''Tis lovely, everyone. Come on, jump in – you scaredy-cats.'

'Harry! Don't be such an idiot!'

Laughter.

They were watched.

They were laughed at.

'Did you ever see the likes of it. Plebs, I'm thinking!'

They had a trailer for the cruiser. Every now and then it sailed up and out of that dead-end road, to be gone for a weekend or weeks.

On calm summer Sundays it bobbed for hours at a distant spot on the lake, restless in the water's rhythm, Nena and Aaron strolling on the road with the au pair.

Her sudden turn in the bed wakens me – she's half lying on my body, listening.

'Sh!' She has heard him, all is quiet now, but she has heard him. She is never wrong, like a fox sensing fear. I have heard nothing, but I know what is coming: a night of walking and waiting, of cold and boredom. Lying there, trapped by her warm, listening-stiff body, I wonder how long it will last tonight.

Then I hear him, braying out the usual song, every dog in his wake howling out. He is without shame: no demand on him now to protect or pretend.

'Come on. Get ready.'

Up and out we go, out into the night. It is dry tonight. We have our coats; we always have our coats with us. There are so many things to be done with a coat besides simply wearing it: you can lie on it, spreading it to soften out tree roots or protruding stones, a bit for her, a bit for me; if the night is warm, it can be balled to make a pillow, the trees' canopy trapping warmth which is comfortable to lie out in for a while without something over you, lying there, catching glimpses of stars through the swaying tops of the trees; nights of wind with moon and racing cloud being my favourite.

It is dark but dry tonight as he sings and sways and swings his way down the dead-end road, so we do what we usually do on such nights: we head straight across to Healy's gateway, swinging quickly to the right, feeling our way along the high stone wall, until we reach a point directly opposite our house. We sit there on two, large, moss-covered rocks which once toppled from the structure of the wall. We can hear him, but cannot see him.

He says: 'No lights! Ha! No lights to welcome a man home after his hard day – 'hat?'

She is shaking, as she usually does. We hear the gate open, we hear the gate close, we hear the door open, we hear the door close. The dogs are quieter. We will wait. She will be silent. I will be silent, too. At some point during the night she'll ask me to run over and see if he's in bed.

We used to know when he'd gone to bed by the fact that the light would be switched off, but he tumbled to this, ever after leaving the light on when he'd gone to bed.

It all seemed like a game, like something the Famous Five would get up to, an adventure: waking from sleep, being silent and quick, running and hiding and not being afraid, shaking with fright-laughter and having to bite down on my tongue in order to stop.

At first we hid in the coal shed at the back of our house, a small shed, a dark shed. That first night we could hear him bawling out her name, 'Mary', plaintive, then angry. He was standing at the front door. Slowly he staggered and stepped back to the coal shed, everything about him heavy and deliberate – his breathing, the smack of his lips, his footfall. He said: 'Come out, you bitch ya, I know you're in there. Come out!' He took a few steps forward. We heard him skid and pitch on the loose coals, swearing as he struggled for his balance, staggering back to the yard. He said: 'Ha! By Jaysus, wait'll I get you, wait'll I get the pair of you. I'm telling you.'

He shuffled off, stopping to piss at the corner of the house. Half an hour later the light went off and we went in.

The shelter of the coal shed ended the night he splashed a bucket of water into the shed, drenching us both. The shock of the cold water made me scream. He said: 'Ha! I knew it!'

She slapped my face, twice.

He laughed and laughed, coughing and hawking, pissing, then farting. I hated him.

That's when we first went for the shelter of the trees. He came home that night, going straight to the back of the house, two buckets of water in his hands. Ten minutes later he was roaring out her name, cursing her, threatening her, pleading with her, swearing at her. In the morning we saw the flood of water in the coal shed, a black stream trickling into the yard. She didn't smile or smirk or act as though she'd just won a battle in their dirty little war. Her face was simply sad.

Going off under the trees was exciting, much more exciting, a real adventure because you could meet rats or bats and other such things – anything.

She said: 'Thank God for the trees.'

The first night tip-toeing through Healy's gateway, I stopped her, wondering what would happen if the Healys came up their drive or down the road.

She said: 'The Healys are in bed. They go to bed around eleven.'

'But there's a light on.'

'That's the bathroom. There's always a light on there, so there is.'

Though sheltered beneath the trees, it soon became cold just sitting there, feet numbing first, a freshness then a coolness creeping up along the body, causing a shudder, and another, then a shiver. She said: 'Come on, let's take a look.' That's when she'd give me a leg up to look over the wall in order to see if the light was out at our house. I said: 'Naw! Not yet.'

'Let's take a walk so as to warm up.'

At first those walks were to the lake and back. Sometimes we'd scurry as far as the crossroad and back, keeping our heads low and moving quickly, hoping for invisibility in our briskness. If the night was wet, we stayed put, hugging close to the body of a tree, seeking its shelter, glad for dryness, ignoring the cold, grateful for small mercies.

The night he left the light on was wild with wind and rain. The trees bowed, now this way, now that way, a noise way up high, a sea sound. We were getting wet, splashes of water being tossed from the leaves, wetting our heads and shocking our necks, larger drops than raindrops, swollen drops slowly spooned from leaf to leaf. We had made a number of quick dashes to the wall: the light was still on.

It was a Friday night, he'd been home earlier than usual, more drunk than usual. She'd been caught unawares, dancing into her coat as he swayed at the doorway. He said: 'Clear out, you bitch ya, clear out to fucking hell altogether! Go on out a that, you fat, fucking old cunt – there was never much good out of you, anyway. Go on out a that!' He kicked her as she passed, falling back against the wall; I darted through that gap, the door banging on our backs.

The wait was long, the wind was hard, the rain was cold. Not long after we'd started our sad vigil, Healy's car came up the driveway, headlights sucking in the rain as it poured. We knew both had gone in the car because we'd seen a pair of bodies dance under the portico and into the garage. Up the garage door went, the world before it flooded with light, rain sucked by it, out came the car with two handles of light, the door behind drooping slowly like a sleeper's eyelid, the light within waning. Everything had stopped for those few moments: there was no cold, no wind, no rain, no darkness, our attention had been held by the scene before us, our misery deadened, forgotten in that bright, brief interlude. I stayed looking at the house, remembering rooms of warmth and Michelle and the hot spice of the food and how it had made my nose run.

She said: 'Let's have another look and see if the light's out.' It wasn't. We were wetter for having looked. Her hair was wet, slick against her head, making her face bigger, eyes bulging, lips thicker. I couldn't read that face. 'I'm cold.'

'And what d'you think I am! Hot, is it? Ha?' Her face was large and naked. She was shaking. Her eyes remained fixed on my face, darting eyes, eyes travelling all over my face. She grabbed my arm, head and shoulders jerking forward before I realised that I was expected to follow her in a run, a dash through the trees, then onto the tarmac drive – shiny-black with wet.

There was a tension-pull between our arms, I was trying

to stop her, fearful for a moment. She drew me on. As we came closer to the house, I guessed where we were heading. The side door to the garage had been left open, a cane of light standing by the wall. In she pushed me before her, closing the door, both of us standing there dripping and blinking in the sudden, sharp brightness.

It was warm. There was a faint drone, a hum. We could hear the wind, the rain ticking against the garage door. It was a double garage. Mrs Healy's car was there, looking like a body in a double bed, the space beside it empty. We surveyed the place from where we stood, then slowly moved around. It was full of bits and pieces; bicycles and balls and Wellington boots, a lawn-mower, forks and spades, a rake and shovels, stacked bags of moss peat, a bucket or two, deckchairs and a pair of sun umbrellas, a golf bag with shiny clubs and clubs covered in colourful socks.

'There! We could sit it out on them for an hour or so.' She was pointing to the deckchairs. It took me a moment or two to realise she was planning on sheltering in Healy's garage. I was relieved, but worried.

I said: 'But what if the Healys come back?'

She was already opening out one of the deckchairs. 'It's Friday night – they're never back before twelve. Come on, get yourself a chair, and take that wet coat off you. Hurry on.'

I followed her to the back of the garage, deckchair in hand, to a spot directly past the stacked bags of moss peat, a secluded spot, hidden from view by the stacked bags, the bags in turn hidden by Mrs Healy's car. We hung our coats on the handles of the shovels and spades and settled in our chairs, side by side, silent. I sneezed, and in doing so caused the deckchair to bounce, its back collapsing to a semi-reclining position. I juggled immediately with the arm rests, eventually having to stand up, pulling the back of the chair upright. It worked. I lifted the arm rests, letting them slide backwards and down went the back again. She said: 'How'd you do that?' With the hum and the warmth and the exhaustion we soon fell asleep, lying back in our deckchairs.

It was too late to move, besides, we were too stunned to do so when the garage door began its noisy climb. We managed to raise the backs of the chairs and sit up straight as the car glided into its place, like children in the classroom when the teacher walks through the door, headlights fading to darkness. Both doors opened almost together and banged shut almost together.

' ... as if John would ever agree to such an outrageous proposal ...' Her voice. Cloc. Cloc. Cloc. Footsteps.

'When a person's dipped to such ...'

Darkness as the door shuts, the lights switched off. The car's engine clicking, cooling. A brief belly-laugh from my mother, rising gently to a volley of hoots.

It was dawn before she and I finally crawled to the lighted window, the noise of wind and rain allowing us to be more daring than we cared to be, crawling right up to the window. Nothing. Easing the door open. Nothing. Just one danno bottle standing by the range: he'd been to bed early. He'd been to bed hours ago; he'd probably been to bed before the Healys had gone out.

We sheltered for many an hour in Healy's garage after that first night. She knew their movements well, when they were in, when they were out, when to expect them to leave, when to expect them to arrive back; she knew Mrs Healy sat in a room at the front of the house most week nights, sifting through papers, bundles of paper; she'd be there for two hours, maybe three, finishing usually around nine o'clock, then a shower in their bedroom bathroom. She knew Mr Healy played golf on Thursday afternoon, that Nena had violin lessons on Wednesday after school, that Mrs Healy played badminton on Saturday morning, taking the children for their riding lessons in the afternoon, that they went out together most Saturday nights, occasionally on Friday nights, but seldom on Sunday; knew when they got up, had meals, when they went to bed, when the lights went out.

There were many nights when we stayed in the garage, the Healys going about their business in their house, her face bright and alive as we sat there on the deckchairs. Knowing they were there, we'd make our way up to the garage via the pathway from the lake, though occasionally she'd grip my hand and pull me quickly down the driveway, taking cover at one or two trees, her body heaving, pulling for air as she stood with her back to the wall in the garage like a gangster being chased, her eyes bright.

She sat in Mrs Healy's car, back seat, passenger seat, driver's seat, touching everything, going through every-thing in the glove compartment, smelling what she could; the same with his car. She took the golf clubs from their bag, reading the writing on the head of each, testing their weight, practicing a swing: 'Hi! Betty, take a look!' She wheeled their barrow, smelled their boots, bounced their balls, swung their rackets, touched their stuff.

The door was shut one night, her body colliding against it as it failed to yield to her pull, senses unable to react quickly enough to the new situation. She ran off, off down the pathway to the lake; I decided to run, too. She was rol-ling there on the grass by the lake, swaying, hugging herself, laughing.

She started going there when it wasn't really necessary to do so, nights when he wasn't drunk, fine nights when he was; there were nights when she tossed and turned in the bed, getting up, getting dressed, leaving without me, returning hours later, breath quick, body cold.

On the nights we had to be there, because of rain and him and cold, she'd sometimes leave me sitting alone on my deckchair, going off by herself to prowl around the house.

My father and my mother became shameless: it was like a duel. When he came home roaring drunk on a bright spring evening, too bright for us to dare our usual walks, to dare visit our usual haunts, she walked up that road with me by her side, the road he'd just come roaring down. She walked solemnly, moving neither too quickly nor too slowly, her attitude like that of one walking the aisle to the altar for communion, conscious of eyes. This I hated. They all saw me: they'd all seen him, heard him.

It was the same on Sunday afternoon. No shame then, no shame at all. We met more people, neighbours strolling to and from the lake. If they could turn from us, they would, feigning interest in another neighbour's shrub or flower, or tying the shoe of a child, unable to look her in the face. If they had to speak, it was: 'Hello. Nice day. Lovely day, thank God ...' walking quickly by, believing they were doing her a favour with their blind eye. They'd pass our house slowly, wanting their fill, eyes averted but ears pricked, hearing him sing, hearing him roar: 'Up Fianna Fáil.' Looking to each other, eyebrows raised: 'Sure God help us all.'

They saw us.

They saw us and our pale faces.

They saw the meek walk of the terrorised.

They saw the clothes, too big for one, too small for the other. Never clean, grubby hair and long, dirty nails. Bread and jam for lunch. Tired children struggling to school, in school. Quiet children – too quiet, shy. Children too much together, too much alone. Children who blushed at the mention of their father or mother.

They saw us.

Sister Rose was long and thin, very thin: an angry thinness. Her face was long and thin, as was her nose which had a red tip and was always damp. She always looked cold, mouth moist, slivers of foam gathering at the corners, bubbling occasionally as she spoke. She had the long gait of a farmer's daughter, deep-set eyes, eyes bred of forefathers used to checking the horizon. She hated us. She taught Christian

Doctrine. Her class started with a show of hands by those who'd gone to mass that morning, while she theatrically noted names in a hard-covered notebook. Everyone was embarrassed: those who had raised their hands and those who hadn't. There was never a class where no one got into her 'God Book' as we called it. The question we asked each other before she arrived was: 'Are you putting your hand up today?' No one ever knew what she did with that notebook and the information contained there.

The Presentation Convent. Sisters devoting their lives to teaching the poor. That's where I went for my free secondary education when I was twelve. Crammed classrooms of navy-clad girls, country girls, city girls; country girls with the fawn socks, beret and blazer; city girls with any colour stockings at all, even shameful tights, anorak or duffle coat, and beretless. They laughed at us, with our school books in suitcases. They smoked and talked about boys, hitching up their gymslips as they passed through the convent gates, laughing and squealing. A glut of girls shuffling between the main school building and prefabs for Latin or Art or French or Science, a glut of knowledge offered by teachers with strained faces, overwhelmed by the numbers to be educated for free, streaming according to their own likes, favouring the bright and the well-bred.

She sent me there on the first day with ringlets in my hair, beret on my head: like Nena at five.

No one spoke to me.

By the time I was fourteen she'd stopped going for those walks, had stopped leaving the house when he arrived home drunk, or at least had begun to do so. There were nights when she did stay. There were nights when she did leave. There were nights of heavy rain or dense cold when she left, nights of soft breezes or a harvest moon when she stayed. He was as drunk on one night as the other. I cannot remember the type of night it was when she first decided not to leave on his drunken arrival. I remember my fright. I had a sexual climax. I sat there, pressing the pulsing lips of my vagina against the rise of that hollowed-out part on the seat of wooden chairs. He was getting closer. She was not moving.

I rocked back and forth. I said: 'He's coming.'

'Let him.'

He stood stock-still in the doorway, shocked at the scene before him, his mouth open, eyes fixed on her, hers fixed on the range. He turned to me, blinking, mouth still open. I looked at the shoe of my swinging foot. Haltingly, he recommenced his song, taking it up at the beginning, sidling into his bedroom.

We walked the roads on many occasions after that night, and when it happened again and again that she didn't leave on his arrival, it came as no surprise: there was no more fear.

On his sober nights he'd always gone to bed after eating his dinner, perhaps taking a walk to the lake and back before doing so. After the change in her behaviour, he began to spend more of his sober time in the kitchen, watching the television; she'd be there, too. He'd say: 'Ha! Jay!' – laughing at the antics of cartoon characters, pairs of eyes moving from the television to him to the television again.

'Go on there, Betty, you're the great scholar, tell us how they done that then.'

He never stayed for very long, not unless she reacted in some way to what was happening on the screen. To her 'Tch! Tch! Tch!' he'd say: 'Hah! Isn't that awful, 'hat?' – his comment directed at no one in particular. If she chuckled, then he guffawed a split second later, finishing with: 'Ha! Jay! Isn't that a terror altogether?' – mouth and eyes disguised as smiling: mouth and eyes retaining their bitter curve. I'd see him watching her, the bitter curve of his mouth twitching.

As I had walked with her, I also waited with her on those nights she decided not to leave. Neither of us would look up as he stood in the doorway, surveying the scene before him; I'd be reading, she contemplating the fire. Sometimes he reversed, staggering out to the dark. We'd hear him pissing on the pathway, grumbling. Other times he'd open a danno, tapping the cap from it by pulling it against the edge of the windowsill, the kitchen windowsill, where the light was, where we were. We'd have gone to bed before he'd finished. Generally though, he went straight to his room, perhaps downing a danno or two there before eventually going to bed.

He says: 'Can't a man sit at his own fireplace at all, any more?' I cross my legs, move forward in the chair and start rocking. We both look at him, standing there in the doorway. He says: 'Hah?' staggering forward, pitching towards the armchair across from her. Breathing heavily, lips firmly shut, hiccuping gently, he sits there opposite her, legs parted, feet firmly planted on the ground, elbows on his knees, head in his hands. She takes a quick, searching look at the top of his head. He shifts suddenly, pulling a danno from his coat pocket, placing it on the floor between his feet, his eyes remaining focused on it. Just as suddenly he plunges his hands in his pockets again, both hands moving together, fumbling together through the pockets, the right one coming out with the bottle-opener. He opens the bottle, a foam of creamy bubbles oozing out, sucked by him and swallowed down.

She uncrosses her ankles, recrossing them in reverse.

He belches before taking another long suck from his bottle, gulping back, Adam's apple rising and falling, then eases himself back in the armchair, resting the bottle on his knee. 'Haven't you no bed to go to?' He is speaking to me.

I say: 'Mama?'

She does not look up.

That was probably the last time I ever sat up with her, waiting for him to come home. It was the last time – bar one – that she went off into the darkness of the night. She'd say: 'Betty, you may as well get to bed. No point in you staying up.'

128

I'd watch them from the bedroom. I watched because there was nothing to hear, and I stopped watching because there was nothing to see; there was nothing to hear until he started to sing, and there was nothing to see because they both just sat there by the range: a man with a bottle and a woman without a smile.

Curled for sleep, I would lie in that bed on those nights hoping for silence, hoping for sleep, pulling the pillow over my head once he started bellowing those meandering songs, mournful songs, songs about wanting to live again in a time gone by. But this was home: a better place than wandering the roads or skulking in Healy's garage. I was glad of my bed.

Her voice joined his.

I crept to the door to see that, to see her sing, to believe it could be true. I saw her, large as life, sitting there, singing along with him, arms unfolded, hands lying on her lap, legs uncrossed, feet flat on the floor, her face without a frown, without a smile, eyes closed, head thrown back and swaying as she sang out the words. He nudged her foot with his. Her hand lifts and reaches: he passes the bottle to her.

I saw them. I watched them. I saw them drinking together, singing together, never speaking or touching or looking directly at each other.

She'd sup for a while from his bottle, then pass it to him in silence, her grasp at its top, his at its bottom. At a moment chosen by him, he'd pull from his pocket another bottle, smaller than a danno, bought especially for her, opened for her by him. She'd be shy of it, laughing at the expectation that she should drink it all, holding it to the light to view the actual liquid, then dribbling it into a tea cup, sucking it down like him. Her songs were his songs, songs she never sang alone, and when she was silent, she was listening to him, learning from him, mumbling in at a point where she knew or could guess the words.

There were silences, never long, never silent: they'd sup

and suck, belch and scratch, she'd poke the fire, rattle the kettle or shift a pot, noisy and deliberate; he'd take off his boots, using both hands, like a child, to undo the laces, his chest resting on his knees, huffing and puffing and fucking Jesus, settling back again in the chair, taking up a bottle, taking up a song; she'd settle, too, her voice joining his.

But if he remained silent, no song tonight, sucking from his bottle, staring straight at her, then she came to bed. She was usually the first to leave anyway.

I was tired of it all. Into the room she'd sneak-stumble, stripping for bed in the darkness, deadened by alcohol, movements slow and awkward, rolling heavily into a deep, sudden sleep, cross-faced and noisy. Occasionally she was enlivened, animated almost, quietly laughing to herself, gay, stretching her body, rolling her body, spreading her arms and legs, doubling up, folding out, drawing my body to hers, her lips on my neck, my face to the wall.

I am awakened by the light. Their singing has been stopped for a while. I've been expecting her, but have fallen asleep. I blink up at the shapes in the doorway, swaying shapes. Someone has switched on the light in the bedroom, blinding my eyes shut. I look towards the floor. His feet are bare, thin legs standing behind hers, her body leaning against his. They sway. They rock. His hand across her belly, the other fanned across her left breast, pressing fingers buried in the brown of her jumper. She moans. He winks at me. Her face is stupid, eyes half-closed, mouth half-open, words bumbling out of her. She looks as though she is going to be sick. I sit up, slowly. She sags. His hands tighten on her body, keeping her on her feet, his stance firm and steady, legs trapping hers.

He says: 'Get out!' She says: 'Don't ...'

'If you know what's good for you – move.'

'Mama?'

He kneads her breasts, pulling her closer to him, rocking

her, squeezing her, rubbing his jaw against hers. She moans.

'Get the fuck out of here, you ugly, fucking bitch.'

I leave. He bangs the door on my back, he bangs it hard, so hard that it bounces open.

I watch. I see them. Him. Her, lying across the bed on her belly, feet dangling to the floor. I see the brown stain of shit on his shirt-tail. He pulls at her skirt, tugging it down. It doesn't come. Hands rush to her waist, fumbling for a clasp, a button, a zip, something.

'Fuck!'

He shoves up her skirt, pulls her knickers down, down, down and out of one leg. He kneels before her, parting her fat, white legs, sucking air between his teeth, kneading the flesh of her thighs and her arse, pulling her forward and sucking her hairs. She lifts on her arms, her head rising, mumbling. He stands, fixed between her legs, pushing her down on the bed. He leans over her, supporting himself with one hand, the other fumbling under his shirt, pulling himself to her, pressing himself down on her, thrusting himself at her, into her, twisting.

She moans. She groans. He starts. I hear the slapping of their flesh. She groans. He grunts. Gradually his body bends down on hers, his rhythm becoming faster, the white flesh of his arse flashing from beneath the leaping tail of his shirt. Beneath him, she manages to lift her head just high enough, allowing her vomit to spray past the spot where her face must lie.

She did not get up the next day, nor the next, nor the day after that. She did not eat. She did not drink. The room stank. She stank. She was naked. She did not speak. She did not communicate by nodding or shaking her head, shrugging her shoulders or gesturing with her hands. I searched her eyes for answers to my questions: there was nothing. She pissed in the bed. By the third day the whole house smelled of that room. The place stank. He sat through it without

131

comment, eating dinners, singing songs. Philomena said I should get the doctor.

Saturday was the fifth day. He got up late that morning, as usual, left for town in the afternoon, came home late that night, drunk, as usual.

The procession of cars started to arrive at Healy's around seven o'clock. We could hear the music of their party. Merry music. Merry people laughing. Merry people calling out greetings – 'Hello!' – to each other. Car doors closing merrily. Everything merry because of the music. Lights on all over the place. The party was at its height when he stumbled through the door, the kitchen filling with the beat of music and the cackle of voices from the lawn, becoming muted again when he closed the door. Philomena and I were sitting in the kitchen, having washed Mary and Amanda for tomorrow's mass and sent them to bed. We'd been talking about her, at least Philomena talked; she spent the evening speculating on what could be wrong with 'Mama'. I listened, pretending innocence to her and to myself, taking comfort in that, wavering between two worlds. I could not tell her what I'd seen five nights ago.

I said: 'It's all his fault.'

'How?'

'He's always drunk.'

'Yeah! I know.'

The smell of the room filled the kitchen when she opened the door. Philomena and I were about to leave for bed, going to the room in which the four of us then slept. He'd just begun his stagger across to the chair by the range. She stood for a moment at the door, then tottered to the centre of the kitchen. She was dressed in her Sunday-best coat, head bare, held to one side, like one listening, she was barefoot, her hands making short, jerky movements, as though beating time to the music we could faintly hear. The fact of her presence was just registering with us when she launched towards the front door, heavy, unsteady steps, like those of a child trying to walk after spinning and spinning, twirling around, playing with the world.

He said: 'Let her off, the bitch.' An instant of music and cool air filled the room before the door banged shut.

I was with her in my mind at all those usual places on that night. I wondered if she dared to go as far as the garage, wondered if she shivered with the thrill of doing so, or did she simply stay by the trees, watching. I shivered with the thought that she might actually go right up to the house and peep through windows. There were cars everywhere; she could hide behind them, listening to people that came and went. Even if she stayed in the garage, she could still see and hear a lot of what was going on.

I shivered. I sat up in bed among my sleeping sisters: I'd remembered she was barefoot. You couldn't walk beneath the trees without shoes, what with stones and roots, she could not go down the pebbly path to their boat-house. She could not stay outside for long without something on her feet.

All I could do was wait for him to go to bed, then quickly switch off the light in the kitchen, letting her know she could come home. I waited and waited, and on and on he sang, pausing between songs for sucks from his bottle. It was two o'clock in the morning when I eventually had the chance to switch off the light. People were beginning to leave the party by then, cars filing up that dead-end road. She would wait until they were all gone, I thought. So I listened to the cars, at first only hearing them as they passed our house, then hearing them start up at Healy's house, straining my ears to hear; cars going by in volleys of twos and threes at first, lessening to ones and twos, then solo cars speeding past, the road to themselves. The night outside became silent. I could hear him snoring in the room next to ours, the tick of the clock in the kitchen, my sisters' breathing, the flick of my eyelash on the pillow.

While it was established that the fire was deliberately started, it was never established whether or not it was by my mother's hand. We read in the *Limerick Leader* how persons unknown had taken a petrol can from the garage, the one used for the lawn-mower, sprinkled the fuel at the front and back door of Healy's house, setting the place on fire. Mr Healy saved his family by breaking the dining-room window. He was quoted as saying: 'The damage would have been far less if I'd been able to phone for the fire brigade before leaving the house.' As it was, he had to run to a neighbour's house, getting them to drive him to another neighbour who had a telephone.

The headline read: *Fire and Tragedy in East Limerick.* The tragedy concerned the woman's body taken from the lake on the morning after the fire. The Gardaí had discovered it while combing the area for clues to the mysterious fire. Foul play was not suspected. The woman was naked beneath the green coat she'd been wearing: found as he had left her. Nor was it believed that any connection existed between the two incidents. She was described as a local woman, the mother of four young daughters: our ages were given. Neighbours described her as a quiet woman, who kept to herself: her age was given. The neighbours were shocked. A Garda spokesman stated that they were continuing their investigation into both incidents.

There was a photograph of the lake, the fire-damaged house and my mother on her wedding day. The lake was described as a peaceful beauty-spot and amenity area. Fire-damaged house not set to suffer the fate of the ruin in the background: family will rebuild again as soon as they can.

Beneath my mother a name and number:

Mrs Wallace, 47.

Time passed, years as brief as moments.

Bill Ryan left Krups and Limerick when his father died, never returning after the funeral. I smiled: another victim I thought, it runs in families.

I never hated him. Why should I? I was a little fool, and little female fools deserve bad things done to them. He did me a favour. The bastard.

At twenty-five, I was the respected spinster of the food-mixer line, given responsibilities because I had no responsibilities: no home, no husband, no children; a future for me, though, in making products for the home: kitchen scales and meat slicers, weighing scales and kitchen clocks, perfect promotion material, the perfect supervisor of teenage girls and married mothers, the dependable one, never late or absent, no morning sickness or bothersome babies or mysterious motherly instincts, instincts mysterious to the male and the childless, concentration never dulled by night feeds or teething, no mornings off to go to the school, or afternoons off to go to the clinic.

They all had their different attitudes towards me. The young teenagers, those still on the prowl – without boyfriends, looking for boyfriends – saw me as being strange and right. They'd ask: 'Are you not married? Are you not engaged? Have you not got a fellah?' I'd say: 'I'm a supervisor.' Huddled in groups, they'd say: 'She's right too, so she is,' a defence against the day when they themselves might not have a man of their own, imagination – or something else – unable to offer them a vision of themselves in that grand role of wife.

They would change. As soon as they had their boyfriend, or no longer had their hymen, they'd wonder about me again, wonder about my hymen. They'd ask among themselves: 'Is she a virgin or isn't she?' They'd ask me: 'Was there never anyone special?' Sometimes I'd say yes to that question and sometimes I'd say no. There was no point in being honest: if you can't tell the truth, then you don't tell the truth. Saying yes seemed to satisfy them, the details they needed were few: 'When? ... For how long?' But if I said no, no there was never

135

anyone special, then that was it: I was a lesbian. That satisfied them, too. They'd spend their time watching for the signs, feeling adult and knowledgeable, wary of being alone with me in the cloakroom, watching to see if I was watching any of them. But soon they were in love, growing thin and silent, or fat and silent, worrying no more about the hymen of others, their life becoming too serious.

The first concern of the newly-weds was washing on the line: would they ever be home in time to bring it in before the rain. I'd say: 'There's nothing worse than a line of wet clothes!' They'd agree, telling me of the recent disaster: 'His Levi's on the line for a whole week!'

Their next concern was food, experimental meals full of spice and more spice, laboured over in cute kitchens, kitchens decked-out with cute stuff, cheap stuff bought in cane shops. They'd promise me the recipe even though I'd not asked, a promise never kept.

Ruling the roost were the older married women, cynical women who never bargained for a life spent that long on the production line. Most married in their early twenties, during the mid-1970s: life planned on Lemass' plan. First generation industrial workers, working in the factories their fathers had built. Husband with a job. Wife with a job, with a plan, with a pill, to live a life only half-like her mother's; have a house, a car, two kids, leave the job after the big holiday in Spain.

But the oil crisis came, and in 1982 the wife with the pill and the plan was still working, never having seen the sun of the Mediterranean. Dreams closed down as factories closed down in that recession; husband sitting at home on the reversible, Draylon three-piece suite, master of the remote control, wife in a world of Christmas savings clubs and union-speak: increment! exploitation! entitlement! incentive! labour-intensive! etcetera, etcetera. Sour women, soured by living.

I was afraid of them. They'd speculate on my freedom, not my hymen. They'd say: 'Don't mind Elizabeth! She's far too clever for the likes of us. Wonder how many's been in that flat of hers!'

My direct boss was a man. The foreman. A man ill-prepared to manage a workforce of women. A married man, with a woman of his own at home. As supervisor, he gave me all the dirty work to do. If someone needed pulling up over the quality of her work or time-keeping, then I was the one to see to it. Time-off was dispensed through me also, but official warnings had to be dealt with by him; it took the good out of his day having to 'speak' to any of the women.

We did not like each other: that's how I came to be promoted. I did not like him because he did not like me. I was not 'delicate' enough. He flirted with most of the girls but never flirted with me, nor with those soured bodies.

Perhaps I had the dead eye of a whore back then, a look of knowledge and loss as opposed to wonder: tired of the male.

He and I could lean head to head over production plans, our bodies never interfering with our minds, he could bawl me out over something – anything, and I'd say nothing, nor would I sulk or cry; if I had done so, he might have cared, but I didn't, so he didn't.

My fling with Bill Ryan must have bothered him at the time, though I don't remember; he must have wondered whether I'd weather my storm, must have wondered how he'd cope with a supervisor suddenly gone all temperamental on him. He spoke to me at length on the treatment of colds when I returned after taking a few days off during the worst of that time. He said: 'You've a cold all right,' relief in his voice, continuing on the merits of Lemsip and Disprin and hot whiskey with cloves.

When it became evident that Bill Ryan and I were no longer an item, his attitude towards me changed, with him becoming ever so slightly kinder, even going so far as to offer me a few more days off. He said: 'Y'know, if you ever need a few days ... I mean, it can be helpful to have some time ... If you ever need it, that is, a couple of days, like, here and there ... y'know.'

I said: 'We need to order some more copper wire.'

Three years between endings, Bill Ryan at one end and the death of my father at the other. Twenty-one I was, with no one to give me a key to a door, a key to a family home when Bill Ryan interfered with me and my memories, dangerous memories seeping from a secret box. I shoved him and them together, quickly bundling the lot back in that box, showing a face to the world that was normal and bright, like a child pretending everything's okay after getting a fright while playing with fire – no one can be told about this: it was all their own fault.

The hair I'd curled for the love, for the attention, of Bill Ryan had lengthened by the time of my father's death. New, straight growth pushed the curls forward until they rested on my neck. For a brief period it looked nice like that, natural-looking, like the curls dangling from a baby's head, regaining bounce and body once bunched in a pony-tail. Then quickly it became a lank mass of split-ends. The soured bodies noticed the change but nothing was said, which was in marked contrast to the way in which they reacted on the morning I arrived in with my new hair-do.

'About time for you to knock that girly look off yourself.

'I once had long hair like that, too, y'know.'

'You have to let it go sometime.'

Perhaps it was my fancy, but I often thought I noticed a little gladness on their faces when I caught them staring at my dying hair-do. I kept meaning to have it redone, kept meaning to make the effort to get myself into a hairdresser once again, but it didn't seem important at all. I didn't really care about my hair, about how it looked; once bunched behind my head in a pony-tail, it didn't matter. I was finished with that world.

Philomena sent a message to the factory telling me – and everyone – that my father was dead. The bitch! She thought she could shame me into going to the funeral. This happened a week after she'd been to the factory telling me of his imminent death. I knew what was coming when the foreman asked me into one of the offices. I was suitably shocked, so shocked I did not cry. I accepted condolence, tea and a taxi, and as much time off as I needed.

On my first day of mourning I stayed in bed, mostly staring at the ceiling and wondering what to do with myself for the rest of the week. Next day I decided to do a major clean-out of the bedsit, heaping old magazines and second-hand paperbacks into a refuse sack, the morning spent leafing through them before discarding them. Old clothes I piled in another bag, that skirt, that blouse, that fun-fur and those shoes.

Next day I walked the town, visiting all the shops, stocking up on underwear and books. I had a take-away for lunch, eating it at the bedsit window, watching the world go by. A hearse pulled into view, an empty hearse, a hearse between bodies gliding up the street. I counted on my fingers and only then realised that he was being buried on that very day. I looked at my watch and knew he was in his hole by then, knew that earth had been dumped upon him, and worms would soon begin their work, a fresh grave in the graveyard where I'd played as a schoolgirl, the body beneath the human-humped earth a relative of mine. I wanted to see that shape, his shape, my dead father in the ground. That was the day I had my hair done, not styled or curled or shortened, but much the way it was on the day I'd left home.

Next day was my homecoming.

Sunk in my pain, I saw and felt nothing of the world in which I lived. I survived in routine, relishing the hour of action: time to wash, time to cook, time for work, time to shop, time to sleep, and all the time pain. After giving my mother's death its name, I lived my normal day.

Mr Draper, he of the camel-like, kind eyes, was a person I always avoided: his knowledge was my terror, even on seeing him in the distance I blushed furiously, conscious of what he knew. I thought he hated me, despising me because of my family. He'd been to the lake, been down that dead-end road, seen where I lived, perhaps even knew our cottage, been witness to the decay of a home of a suicide mother. He, too, avoided me. Chance meetings in corridors or the canteen were painful for us both, each equally embarrassed, withholding acknowledgement of each other until the very last moment.

'Elizabeth,' his face serious and shut, like a doctor with bad news.

'Mr Draper,' my heart racing, face burning, my self raging.

Right from the very beginning I watched every move made by Mr Draper: learning to stay out of his way by knowing his ways. I knew what time he arrived at work, where he parked his car, what times he went to the canteen, knew his movements through the factory throughout the day.

It was he who had to announce to me my success in being promoted to supervisor. Three others besides myself had put their names forward for the position when it became vacant. There was no interview. Apparently our merits and demerits were discussed by the foreman, the personnel manager and Mr Draper, who was the assistant manager.

The four of us sat in Mr Draper's office a fortnight after submitting our names; the foreman was there also. I was not embarrassed, embarrassment only came when I was caught off-guard, as it were. Sitting before him in his office was no real bother to me. I looked straight ahead, looking at him without staring, breathing deeply, concentrating on the minutes passing. He spoke, head nodding at each of us in turn, his voice soft and gentle. I noticed a slight film of sweat on his upper lip, visible only when his head tilted in a certain way. When the others giggled at something said, I made a smile. And when they rose to leave, so did I, but suddenly my hand was being grasped and shaken by everyone: 'Congratulations! Congratulations! Congratulations!' Mr Draper

140

slipped his hand over mine, giving it a moist, gentle squeeze, his other hand folding over our joined hands, mine then cupped between his, like a child does in holding a delicate life, like that of a butterfly or a ladybird. He said: 'Well done, Elizabeth. Well done.'

I became supervisor and nothing changed between myself and Mr Draper. We continued to veer off in different directions when faced with the prospect of meeting face to face.

I pondered that handshake, pondered the kindness I'd felt, or thought I felt. I did not know what to do with it, did not really trust it, did not have the ability to acknowledge it.

His face opened and closed on the morning I spoke to him in the canteen. I had followed him there, timing my move so as to be right behind him in the queue, a long queue.

It was a time when I was wiser, a time when I needed to be beyond pity, a time when I realised that I'd lived too long in the shadow of a shame that was not mine. I then saw his kindness in avoiding me as plain rudeness, an enforcement of the feeling that I should still feel shame.

I said: 'It's not a bad day for the time of year, is it?' I nodded to the world beyond the canteen window.

'Yes! No! Yes! Yes, indeed it is a nice day now. A nice day.'

My eyes held his for just a moment, then travelled to the world beyond, both of us looking in the same direction. Eye to eye contact had been brief, broken by him; his a look of surprise, followed by questioning, while mine was a look of defiance, wide-eyed and steady, to his wide-eyed and darting. I had hoped, but never believed, that he would continue the conversation, half-hoped that maybe he'd drop the old guard, leaving me in, or out, whichever way one looks at it. He didn't speak, didn't say anything else. I didn't care, I was having fun with the silence, thrilled by the nervousness I could detect coming from him – the shuffle of a foot, the winding of his watch, the counting of his change, the shuffle of a foot.

I said: 'Although, while in Spain this year, I often found myself longing for a day such as this. Wasn't that crazy?' I laughed, my face full on his. It was a dying-bright autumn day, cool, the canteen suffused in its sad tones.

'Were you there with many others? I mean, did you go with a group from here, I mean, you know?' The question surprised me, at least the depth of thinking behind it caught me off-guard, as it were; I had been expecting something more general, his laugh maybe, maybe something like 'you should have enjoyed the sun while you had it'.

I had been to Spain on my own. I had been to many places on my own. The first had been a coach tour around England; ten days on a luxury bus, nights spent in average hotels, never sleeping in the same bed twice, having lunch and tea in various tourist traps: quaint village – home to the house of a long-dead poet; majestic castle – tea-rooms in the dungeon; scenic mountain pass – car-park oasis with toilets and café. Dinner that night in the hotel, maybe, or sometimes I'd make my way to the nearest take-away, eating in my room, wondering about my bedsit, picturing the scene from the window there. I had paid the supplement for travelling alone; had my story all prepared of how my friend had been taken ill at the last moment. Appendix. Nothing serious. Must send back a card.

I was not alone in being alone; that surprised me, pleased me: Noah would not have been amused: lone females on the voyage. Everyone was very nice to everyone on meeting for the first time, 'Hellos' were loud and bright. The initial ice-breaker discussion was on why a coach tour in the first place:

'No worries.'
'Everything done for you.'
'Fresh at the end of the day.'
'More energy for the night.'
'Make new friends.'

'Never stuck in the same place for too long.'

'See all the sights.'

I was one of the youngest there, in my late-twenties at the time, the group comprising mainly middle-aged couples. There were others who travelled alone: a woman not yet in middle-age, no rings on her left hand, cool, crisp and aloof, her lips fixed in a permanent half-smile, even when she nodded off to sleep on the coach. She said 'Hello' to everyone on the first day, never speaking again until saying goodbye at the end of the journey; there was a man in his early thirties, perhaps, always seen with a paperback, he mumbled to himself on the coach, biting his nails, his face turned upon the world fleeing past; there was also an older man, retired, hearty, chatty, rarely looking through the window, poking his face instead through the seats in front of him or through the seat in which he sat, carrying on a loud conversation with the couple there.

I spoke to anyone who spoke to me, though quickly adopting the role of listener: trick of the watchful, the deceived.

I was invited to have drinks with various couples, getting acquainted with her while he was ordering at the bar. She'd hear the story about my friend with the appendix, but only if she asked, otherwise I directed her straight to the topic that would keep both of them going until bedtime: their family.

Gender mix, number of, age and current status were the usual openers, followed by personality type – mostly good, well-behaved children, little evils glossed over, mothered over, all like their father in their cleverness: 'Nearly ten pounds in weight when he was born ... came first in a competition for reciting poetry ... got that from her father's side of the family ... couldn't keep the fridge full when they were teenagers ... never a bit of trouble with him, never ... did take a drink for a time ... stopped after that car ran into his ... still, a drink now and then does no one no harm at all ... college didn't suit her ... wanted to see the world ... have money of her own ... her husband has a very good position in one of those computer factories ... has one of those beepers ... has to be able to be contacted at all times ... very good to her, he is ... still ... the eldest's an accountant ... hopes to have his own firm some day, with the help of God ... always very good with the figures ... takes after his father there ... doing some night-class in computers for the past two years ... finds it hard to come and visit ... still, we can't complain ... he's very good to us ... very hard when you're starting out ... still ... all the same ... has been living with her for a year ... what can you say, I mean ... never met her parents ... she's an engineer of some kind or other ... her own car and all ... still ... not a bit of shame in front of others ... we don't know what the world's coming to ... no morals nowadays ... still ... all the same ... wouldn't you think?

The couples came in two types, those where she did all the talking, while he had all the appearance of listening, and those who finished each other's sentences, tossing bits of remembrance between each other, reconstructing their babies.

From twosome to lonesome twosome they would flit, searching for themselves in each other, looking for the story which resembled their own, finding it, only to lose it again and again, like a dream dreamt but only half-remembered. Earnest face watched earnest mouth speak. I could know from the distance what they were saying, their lips shaped by the name of the child about whom they were speaking: 'John ... Mary ... Michael.' Two by two they'd pass my door at a late hour, back to their room, back to the world they'd left for a while.

I've had many coach holidays since that first one. I like them, like the fact of moving on every day, so much to see, to hear, so many different rooms, with different views, people watching us pass, or shuffle through some interesting museum, seeing us as a party of friends, all together, but as alone as you like. I went to France after the trip to England, other years going to Holland, Belgium and Germany. But Spain was different. In Spain I was on my own, spending two weeks in a holiday apartment, two hot, sultry, Spanish weeks alone in the heat.

I said: 'I took a coach trip there, on my own. But you're never alone on a coach tour. It's a great way of meeting others, making new friends and all that. I've been to many places by coach. Last year I went to ...' Mr Draper listened to my list of delightful trips, attentive, relieved, coins jingling in his hand as he sorted change for his morning coffee and newspaper.

After that first encounter it was never so bad for him when we 'accidentally' met on other occasions. Gradually he became more talkative, less nervous, becoming a little uneasy though if I mentioned anything about, say, back home, his eyes widening, eyebrows pulling together: a warning being heeded. Eventually he stopped avoiding me.

It was time to speak, I needed to speak, needed to say it, to name the truth of my mother's death to someone who already knew that truth, needed to bury my shame.

Mr Draper had a coffee and a read of his paper for a quarter of an hour or so every morning. I'd see him in the canteen any time between quarter past nine and twenty to ten, leaving before the place was invaded by the workers having their ten o'clock tea-break. I waited until I knew he was sitting, until I knew that he was absorbed in his paper, feeling if he saw me, if we looked at each other that I'd fail to speak; I wanted him to be surprised by my presence, his mind full of the news he'd been reading, no time to place the woman before him, perhaps only the name Elizabeth Wallace forming in his mind before I began to speak. I said: 'D'you mind if I join you, Mr Draper?' His eyes widened and blinked twice, quickly.

'Do! Do! By all means, do.'

I sat opposite him. He folded his paper, never looking at me, and when he did look up, he smiled, bringing the cup to his mouth, his eyes looking into it as he drank. I waited until he was finished.

'Mr Draper, I've been meaning to say something, to tell you something for some time now.'

'I thought so, Elizabeth.'

'You did?' The words were out before I knew what I was saying.

'Life hasn't been easy for you, has it?' That made me look at him, really look at him, eye to eye like lovers or enemies about to act.

'Yeah! An alcoholic father and a mother who committed suicide – it's enough for anyone.' I smiled. He smiled. He waited.

'The worst part – d'you know what the worst part is? ... was? ... because I'm over all that now. The worst part is feeling you're to blame.' I took his paper, adding one more fold to it. 'It's people who make you feel like that, y'know, like you've done something wrong, like you're the one who killed your mother, or something.' I unfolded the paper, refolding it in the opposite direction. 'It's in the way they look at you and don't look at you, and how they avoid you whenever they can, like you've got something contagious. Y'know what I mean?' I began to roll the newspaper, making it look like a rolling-pin or a truncheon. 'Everything changed, but my mother couldn't.' I tapped the table with the rolled paper. 'She hated him, y'know. That's why she did it.'

There was a pause, a long pause, but I had nothing more to say. I had said it. He kept his head bowed. When he raised it, his eyes were huge and hurt-looking.

'I was never too sure whether or not you knew about your mother's suicide, Elizabeth. I thought maybe the truth had been kept from you, thought maybe you'd been told she died in the fire that night.' He took a sip from his cup. 'You were so young when it happened – all of you were: that's what I remember most. It was never easy to know how to relate to you, especially when I knew your story – ' I stopped him. 'Part of my story, Mr Draper.'

'Yes.' He paused, searching my face. He blinked. 'Part of

your story. I could never help wondering ...'

The muffled sound of the ten o'clock tea bell became clear and distinct as the canteen doors swung open to the flood of navy-clad girls streaming in for their morning tea, chattering and laughing and calling, chairs scraping on the floor, change jingling. I handed him his paper. We both rose and left.

Spain. Spain was a decision made out of boredom, my thirtieth birthday and boredom. I am a Capricorn, born in the deadest part of the year, a terrible time to face the fact of thirty, to face the fact of ageing. Darkness comes too soon on the day of your birthday when you are a Capricorn. I searched for signs of ageing – wrinkles, sagging flesh, but could not see myself as being any different from the time I was twenty. Flesh beneath my eyes creased when I smiled, but only when I smiled. I had not fattened. Size twelve jeans fitted easily, size ten for days when I felt good and bright and alive – fresh and enlivened after my periods. My breasts were firm, small, with small nipples, my stomach flat, flesh tight on my thighs, blue-pale all over, except my arms, face and hands, which were duller from living in the light of day. I felt still young. I was thirty and still felt young. I was not prepared for that feeling, thought life had been settled, thought nothing would ever change, did not really want change, was comfortable as I was, as I had been, secure in my routine.

The feeling was a feeling of wanting something else: change my clothes, my hair, my face, shed my skin. I had never lain in the sun. I had never worn a bikini, oiled my flesh and lain in the sun.

I had gone through a period after Bill Ryan when I hated my body, dressing it in cheap, dark, loose clothes: garb of woman, the blamed; feeding it on the plainest of the plain, no sugar, no sweets, no salt, skimmed milk in my tea, no meat, no butter, nothing to nourish what I hated. That period ended when my father died, those cheap, dark clothes finding their own grave, too.

147

Baths. Always a shower person, I then loved baths, luxurious, foaming, scented, long, hot baths. When the place was quiet, which varied according to the living habits of the many people who passed through that house, I'd gather together my bottles and lotions, no shyness then of being naked beneath my dressing gown, and go for a bath.

Sometimes I'd stir from my day-dreaming at the window, the room in darkness except for the glow of the street lights. Was I thirsty? Tired? What did I need? Was it very late, or something? Had someone called my name? What did I need? Stretching and yawning, stiff from sitting, I'd strip, knowing I needed a bath. And stripped, I'd move around that room, choose a towel, choose a fragrant oil, or bath foam, or bath soap, moisturiser, lay out fresh underwear on the bed for when I got back, slip on my dressing gown.

Sitting on the side of the bath I'd watch the taps pour, water filling, steam rising. I'd rake my fingers through that foam, checking the water, then turn one tap, the flow from the other modifying the temperature, foam forming like a blanket of snow, drops from a bottle transformed by the rushing water. Into it I'd ease my body, feet dipping through the blanket of foam, body folding down into it, then stretching out in warm, silky, scented water. Along arm and leg, shoulder and breast I'd sponge flesh, liking what I saw: long legs, elegant arms, the blue-pale skin of my breasts; liking what I felt: warm, velvety flesh; how I felt: at ease, feeling supple and lithesome.

There was always a period of stillness before I unplugged the bath, simply lying there, mind vacant, noise within the house quite distant from me. And just before I'd unplug the bath, I'd pull my head beneath the clear water, knees up, head down, the foam dissipated by then, eyes staring through at the ceiling, hair waving above my face, like a silk scarf in a soft breeze. I'd think of a womb, of myself being in a womb, the bath like a womb: wet and contained. I'd lift the plug with my foot, the warm water rapidly deserting my naked body, hair flattening around my face like rats' tails, goose-bumps on my flesh.

For someone who never had the chance to bring her virginity to the communion altar, I felt virginal. I felt virginal because I had never been seen, no one had ever seen my pubic hair or my mature breasts, the curve of my waist. I had been fingered, sucked, fucked, but never seen, never wondered at by another virgin, never had a nervous hand touch me in awe: I was like a used toy in a new box.

I had tried to be seen, had been careful to be careless in wrapping the bathrobe over my naked body, would know who was coming through the front door just as I was about to go for my bath, or leave the bathroom. Just to be seen. My waist – the tight pull of the sash outlining its curve, my neck – a V of blue-pale flesh framed by the robe; my legs, my long legs glimpsed, flashing through as I strode by, or stood standing for some reason in a nonchalant pose at my door, letting someone pass on the stairs, picking up a dropped item. But when they who saw me spoke to me, I froze, reddening all over, stuttering and stammering and scurrying away, even something as simple as saying 'Hello' was an effort for me. Once back in the shell of a room – my room or the bathroom – I'd be ashamed of myself, ashamed of everything about myself: they were laughing at me, laughing at the get-up of me going around the place.

I'd meet other women in their bathrobes, but they looked as though they were going for a bath – hair tossed or pinned up unattractively, mine brushed loose, carefully framing my face. I looked like I was taking a walk, a Sunday stroll in a park.

It took a happy self to be like them.

When I saw the poster in the travel agent's window, on the day of my thirtieth birthday, it wasn't the beach or the sea or the blue, blue sky I noticed: it was her body, her almost-naked body, its curves, her confidence as she reached for a bright ball in the air – it could have been the sun. I noticed the

149

people in the background who were watching the woman at her game. I noticed his body too, noticed the straight, strong lines of her male playmate.

I had known many who had been to Spain, mostly honeymoon couples and the occasional group of girls off for two weeks of sun, sea and fun, fun, fun, all arriving back suitably burned and tanned and wearing the place-name T-shirt or sporting shoulder bags of bright, stiff leather. The Costa del somewhere or other were the usual destinations, more thought given to cost than location.

When I told the woman at the travel agents I was planning a holiday in Spain, she immediately began listing off the usual places, circling rates for the July-August period with her ballpoint pen on the glossy page of a brochure. I asked her if I could see the map of Spain, wanting to know exactly where I was going. She referred me to the front of the brochure, telling me to have a seat and take my time; I told her I'd bring it with me.

Back in my room I chose an island, liking an island because of its completeness. Ibiza is a complete place, not simply a spot on the coastline of a continent. It looks a little like my island, more narrow than broad, with its capital on one coast and a beautiful bay on the coast opposite. I chose to go to that island, deciding to spend two weeks in a self-catering apartment on that bay, San Antoni Abad.

I lay in bed for two whole days after arriving there, utterly sick at the decision I'd made. I was probably suffering from travel exhaustion, dehydration and hunger. My doubt began on the coach drive to San Antonio. I'd a headache from the sun, its piercing light bouncing off the all-white buildings in Ibiza town, with the noise of car horns everywhere, hot air pressing down. At the airport we'd been grouped according to tour operator, who in turn sorted us according to where we were staying. Most on the coach were British and young: couples holding hands, she looking romantic, he looking adventurous, cliques of young men and cliques of young women already drinking the alcohol purchased at the Duty Free. One of those young women sat beside me, having no other choice but to do so. Once we were out on the motorway and speeding along, she went to join her friends, standing for the remainder of the journey. I sat alone, my face turned on the glaring, alien landscape, body swaying stiffly with the motion of the bus, legs crossed, thighs pressed tightly together, turmoil between my legs.

The amount of green to be seen there surprised me; gnarled, ancient-looking trees, standing alone or in small pockets, dotted a landscape which was a mixture of grey and dust-green, struggling-green, not like the lush-green of home, the land pocked-marked with bald patches of sandy earth. And everywhere, flat-roofed, brilliantly white-washed houses, more like outhouse than dwelling house; tall, crooked trees shading them, the sandy earth stretching right up to their walls; windows, small and shuttered, doorways recessed, a cool, shady entrance.

The dark-dressed people of those white-washed houses were the same peasant people to be seen in any peasant setting; the old women in their long, dark clothes, heads hidden in dark shawls, could have been the sisters of Peig from the Blaskets, even their weathered, withered faces – toothless mouth, deep-set eye – held a trace of something, of someone familiar. The men, too, in their dark clothes, berets on their heads, had a familiar look as they bounced along on faded-white carts pulled by faded-white donkeys, thin, sand-coloured dogs following behind. I felt at ease as we passed through that slow, ancient, almost-familiar world, that ease dying as the bus slowed on the outskirts of San Antonio.

I was then in a world of high, white buildings, cheek by jowl in row after row, modern buildings without beauty. I felt cowed by them, disturbed by the ritzy atmosphere of the place, flesh everywhere I turned: swinging arms, striding legs, bare chests of men, soft bellies of women, swaying shoulders, cleavage, biceps, calves, thighs, oily flesh – lush, like berries ripening; people drifting along sidewalks, bodies weaving through bodies. I smiled at that parade – a physical act without emotion, face muscles holding in check a rising anxiety.

My apartment block was only four storeys high, the Marian apartments, four streets back from the man-made beach, cheap while not the cheapest. On reaching my room, which was on the top floor, I immediately drew the curtains, stripped to my underwear, crawled onto the bed and cried until I slept. I cried for everything, but most of all I cried for myself; I cried for Saturdays and Sundays during which I never spoke, for nights spent listening to the world having fun, for the knot gathering between my eyebrows, for my pot-plants hidden from light until my return, my mug, plate, bowl, knife, fork, spoon, for tears in my eyes when I awoke in the night-time, dreamtime, my wrinkling flesh, the blood from my womb.

I am naked on the stairway of the house, my body warm and scented from the bath. So many people! I must weave my way through them, rubbing my breasts and buttocks against them as I squeeze past, tongues darting into my mouth. My moist mouth. My wet mouth. Mouth wet from water.

Cool hands linger on my body, kneading my breasts, buttocks, stomach, hard bodies pressing against mine.

I take a hand, a male hand snatched from the crowd; we pull our way past the others, alone on our way to my room. He stands behind me, arms above me, hands pressed against the door as I fumble a key into the lock, feeling the heat from his body, feeling his body move, his knee between my legs, hot tongue-tip on my neck. I laugh. The key softens, dissolves, drips from the lock, drops like tears falling at my feet. His hand cups the door-knob, twisting it: it does not move. He walks away, skipping down the stairs.

I shiver. Cool air then wafts about my body, air from the

room as the door slowly swings open. I turn to call him, but have no words with which to fill my mouth. There is laughter, loud laughter coming from my room. I take a step forward, looking in there, seeing it all as though for the first time: bed, chair, wardrobe, pink geraniums on the window, huge pink blooms nodding as though laughing. I rush to them, snapping off the blooms one by one, but the laughter remains, is getting louder. I push the flowerpot from its spot, earth and leafy stems spilling around my feet, feet still wet from the key's tears. I roll the blooms between my hands, pressing them firmly, their mass dwindling, being reduced to pulp, feeling sticky, then moist between my palms, juice dripping through my pale fingers, a red liquid splashing onto my body, dripping slowly down my legs.

Dreams like that were to be part of my sleep for those two days. Laughter would sometimes awaken me and I'd know that I'd not been dreaming, the sounds around me too real to only be in my head; other times I'd awaken, wondering about the door I'd just heard bang shut, but there was only silence and heat and my heavy body, more tears, more dreams.

On the third day I awoke, not stirred by light or noise but by smell, a heavy smell, neither sweet nor sour. Familiar. At the same time I became aware of the stickiness between my legs, of the dampness on which I lay. I had had my periods, had been bleeding for those two days. I felt weak, thirsty, dirty as I opened various doors looking for the bathroom, my movements slow and determined. Once standing in the shower, I let the tepid water rain hard upon my stale body, stripping my knickers, squeezing them, faded blood streaming between my fingers, my body washed without soap, like one standing in the rain.

By the end of the first week I'd managed to start living in that warm, sunny world. My first meal was in the snack bar of the apartment block: *agua mineral, una ensalada, pan*. The swimming pool was just beyond the door of the snack bar, screeching and splashing noises filtering through to me as I ate.

What I needed first were some different clothes, something more suitable than heavy jeans and hot runners, the clothes which usually got me by on my coach trips. I needed something cool and light, something bright to do battle with the heat of the sun. I bought a dress, a white, light, cotton dress, my first dress since communion day, loose and long, hanging past my knees, with wide uncuffed sleeves to the elbow, a thin draw-string at the waist, buttoned from there up to the collar; and shoes: *alpargatas*, shoes of straw and hemp, flat and airy.

I felt well in that dress, in those shoes, cool, confident that I looked elegant. Not sexy. Not beautiful. Simply elegant. It was given in that look from older men, those who imagine you on their arm in a crowded place, their eyes never travelling over your body, remaining instead on your face, measuring your height against theirs, seeing you as a woman, satisfied that all trace of the giggling, crying girl is gone: practised and independent. It was there also in the look given by younger males, those who stepped quickly to one side, allowing me pass on a narrow sidewalk, or who dropped their voices when I sat nearby in a café, intimidated by the presence of a woman, her curves hidden: more practised than they. Although, there were some among them who delighted in performing exaggerated acts of chivalry, as much a challenge to my apparent indifference as a macho display before friends.

I bought a wide-brimmed straw hat with a pale-yellow ribbon around it, sunglasses, too, and a straw basket which hung from the shoulder.

By the end of the first week my body had begun to colour, skin smooth from all the sun cream and use of after-sun moisturiser following my shower. I'd spend some time in the mornings, an hour perhaps, sunning myself on the furnished sun terrace by the pool. It was usually quiet at that time, too early for the night hawks, too limited for those seeking others, who chose instead to go to the beach, leaving behind those who'd just arrived, pale Northerners shy of their pale bodies, people like myself.

I had been a little tense the first time walking across the sun terrace in my bikini, so conscious of male and female eyes evaluating my body. Taking a deep breath, I focused on a sunbed in a quiet part of the terrace, heading for it without looking to the left or the right of me. Ten minutes later I witnessed the entrance of three noisy girls in black bikinis, all eyes turned on them, eyes that had been on me a moment before, my eyes on those who watched, their interest held for a moment, then back again to themselves – more oil on leg or stomach, next page of a book turned, others not watching at all, serious faces with closed eyes, willing the sun on their flesh. That was the business of the place: sun on flesh. Semi-naked bodies without allure. Plain and simple. Nothing else mattered at all.

I'd shower after my morning in the sun, smoothing after-sun moisturiser all over, hands kneading flesh rarely touched – between my thighs, over my breasts, along my neck, down the length of my legs. Naked, I would lie on top of the bed, my body cooling in air shifting through the open window, sounds from the street – slow-moving people and the occasional slow-moving car – filtering up, my mind lulled by that hum in the heat. I'd awaken feeling fresh and hungry, ready for the world beyond my apartment, ready to wear my dress, glasses, hat, shoes, putting some magazines in my straw bag.

To the promenade on the bay-front is where I'd go. I liked it there. It was a place always packed with people, lost-looking couples meandering through crowds of lost-looking couples, café beside café, dark within, with clusters of white plastic tables and chairs at door fronts, shaded with colourful umbrellas. Orange. Blue like the sky, like the sea. Yellow. Cool white. Fun stripes of many shades. Groups of colour like those of a map, defining territory between cafés; all-white buildings with half-moon balconies at first-floor windows, surrounded with ornate, black wrought iron railings, from which pots of blood-red geraniums spilled, or signs advertising Pepsi or Coke, chilled, within; people sitting at those tables, either couples or gangs, a profusion of colour in the clothes they wore – lime-greens, bright-pinks, pale-blues, dazzling-whites, the proud dome of nipples pressing against light material, faces wrapped in mystery, eyes hidden by dark glasses.

I usually lunched at that place, spending much time in staking out a vacant table in a suitable spot, preferring to sit facing the promenade, but sitting well back near the wall of the café. When the waiter came I'd nod at him, saying: '*Menu, por favor*', which meant one wished to have the dish of the day, which normally consisted of grilled fish, served with salad and fried potatoes. It was my main meal of the day, so I ate heartily, one of my magazines propped before me, having a coffee, perhaps two later, which I sipped slowly, watching the world go by.

The entire promenade was flanked by a park area, tall trees, tubs of flowers, benches in shady spots, more concrete there than grass, yellowed grass, jaded from the struggle to survive. The focal point was the fountain. Like the welcome crackle of a fire on a cold, cold day, its water splashed and bubbled, a sensation of coolness in that raining sound, the benches nearest it usually taken, hot tourists cooling, like weary travellers warming at a fire.

I liked to sit there, especially after my lunch. It was the place the local youths came to show-off in front of tourist girls; lying beneath trees in small groups, the occasional mock-wrestle breaking out, or languidly kicking a soccer ball from one to the other, cackling loudly, all dressed in tight, faded jeans that were a year or two behind the current fashion, white T-shirts and white runners, an American style which didn't quite work. Others who were there came to sit on the benches or lie in shade as they ate take-away food or refreshed themselves with cans of Coke or mineral water, feet freed from shoes or sandals for a while, couples hugging the shade of a tree as they changed film in cameras, some came to nap on the grass, glad toes twitching in the sun, others smoked, propping their bodies against the dish of the fountain, some read, some watched.

One day as I walked there after my lunch, satisfied and lazy, moving slowly in the heat, what seemed like bleeding flowed between my legs. Disgusted, I went to the nearest toilet, discovering a white mucus glued to my knickers and the tips of my pubic hair. Touching the stuff on my knickers, I smelled its acid tang from my fingers, putting my hand down there again, touching the hairs, hairs that tingled to the touch, fingers sucked by the mucus-slick, swollen lips of my vagina, one, two, three fingers in up, up, acid smell rising from between my legs, something oozing down my fingers, heart racing, fingers slipping in, slipping out, slipping in again, legs spreading with pleasure, in, out, hairs rubbed wet, slicked down, my slit wide, wider, thick, oozing, palm slippery, stroking, spreading sap, on thighs, on belly, fingers probing for more of everything, doors opening, closing, people's voices, pissing, flushing. I stopped. Hot. Heaving. Shocked. Thirsty. My knickers stuck to me when I pulled them up, so I slipped them off, putting them in my bag. I needed something to drink, quickly.

Standing in line at a kiosk, I was convinced everyone could smell the sap of my body, like a bitch in heat.

If I had been touched, if a male hand had touched mine, I would have pressed my body against his. I thought that.

I sat on a stone bench, greedily sucking from my bottle, aware of a trickle of sweat rolling between my breasts, my dress spread around me, private flesh against the cool stone, hot and damp, legs uncrossed, slightly parted. I did not look at the world going by, instead I pondered my toes released from their shoes, occasionally sniffing my fingers which still bore a trace of my smell despite having been washed and washed.

If it had happened on any other day, I'd probably have allowed the soccer ball roll on its way, too shy to be the one tossing it back to the boys; instead, when the ball rolled into my field of vision – black and white tumbling together – I reached out my foot, stopping its run, holding it there, as though simply resting my bare toes on it, watching it move to the will of my foot. Soon they were there, stopping dead from their run on seeing their ball, colliding together, like a litter of pups on the run stopping on encountering a human. They looked at my hat, face behind dark glasses, dress spread out, feet bare, their ball.

He stepped forward, gesturing to the ball, smiling, spewing out gibberish – late-teens, early twenties, tallish, slim, dark, strong-looking for his age.

I said: 'This your ball?'

He stepped closer, his friends quietly jeering. He said: '*Si! Si!*' I continued to play with it, the spot beneath my foot becoming moist. More chatter from him, spewed from a smiling, moist mouth, light hands gesturing. I twirled the ball for a moment more, then thrust it from me, aiming it to run towards his friends, who jeered loudly then, his face smiling, shoulders shrugging in mock helplessness as they ran off, leaving him with me.

Just for a moment he looked as though his daring might leave him, hands stuffed in the pockets of his jeans, head turned to his feet which toyed with a pebble. He said, shyly: '*Ingles?*' I shook my head with a smiling face, removing my dark glasses: a concession.

Abruptly, nervously, he sat at the end of my bench, drawing a packet of Marlboro from the pocket of his T-shirt, he offered me one and I took it, wondering if he could smell my fingers as they reached towards him.

'I am Elizabeth Wallace. I come from Ireland. Ireland is the island next to England. A green place, with lots of cows and a small population of people.' I smiled at him. He smiled at me. I continued to tell him about my island, nonsense to him, but like the message from the voice of the lullaby singer, he was hearing the truth.

Meandering along like everyone else, we walked the length of the promenade that day, him listening to me as I spoke, parting where we had met, at the bench by the fountain, the place I had sat after wanting more of my own hand.

He was the prop for my fantasies that night, and many nights as I lay naked on top of the bed, second finger, right hand probing that moist tit of flesh I'd discovered that day, much pleasure to be had from the touch, even more from the rhythm which developed, a stroke determined by something within, constant and precise like seconds ticking, tension rising, stiff with wonder, waiting, wanting, like the moment before the release of a sneeze, all senses dead, not seeing, not hearing, the rhythm becoming intense, finishing suddenly in thrusts of pleasure, thrusts of anger.

We met at the same place for the rest of my stay, walking quickly to quiet places to pleasure ourselves, long hours of pleasure. He first kissed me against a tree in the park, a hot, firm, eager mouth and body.

He soon adopted my way of speaking, not needing to be understood, holding my hand, steering me through hot crowds in market places, spewing out chattering words, our bodies in constant collision, nudging against each other. He took me to quiet fields on the outskirts of the town, beneath trees there, opening the wrappers of condoms with his teeth, like a child opening a packet of crisps.

I once saw him kick dust upon an oozing condom, burying his sin in the earth, his face becoming shy on seeing that I had seen him. I kissed him and had him again.

I was always naked beneath the dress, delighting in the cool touch of his hand when we met, him squeezing out my sap, preparing me, then running me to some alley, secluded, against a wall, urgently. Or the dare of walking in a crowd, his fingers probing there, shooting up quickly while the moment allowed, toying with each other among the cover of people.

There were days when we never lay on the ground.

I washed my dress each night, hanging it to dry on the balcony, ready again for the next day, wrinkles disappearing in the sun.

His name was Pedro, and I loved my name in his mouth: 'Eee-lez-e-bath.' He got me to drop the shoulders of my dress, like a Spanish Señorita, opening a daring number of buttons, then rolling the collar over my shoulders, which he suncreamed for me in quiet places, kneading my breasts and back and neck, rocking me with his body.

Sometimes the urgency was mine. I'd be the one hurrying him to quiet, crude places, unbuttoning him, the condom already unwrapped in my hand, like a sticky sweet, thrusting my body against his. Such was the case that day in the ancient church in the old part of the town.

He had taken me there, presumably to show it to me. It was large and dark, with many arches of cool shade. We'd been sitting on the stone steps, refreshing ourselves in the shade, drinking water, my private flesh pressed against the cold stone. I'd been telling him about the churches back home, telling him how steep they were, and grey, built of the same coloured stone as mansions for the rich, prisons for the poor, the courts of law, asylums for the mad and colleges in which the rulers learned. When we rose to leave, I noticed my sap stain on the stone. He noticed it too. His face became shy. I put my tongue in his mouth, but he pulled from me, shaking his head, hands gesturing as if to say 'look where we are, for God's sake!' But I only smiled and knelt before him, his penis in my mouth before he even knew what was happening, sucking him erect, and when he was, I had him in me, quickly, no time for a condom, bareback in the house of God, he rocked and rocked, as any male would, little flakes of dust from that sacred wall gathering on my shoulders.

He pulled from me quickly when he came, buttoning himself up, fast.

I laughed, standing spread-leg against the wall, as he had left me, his semen oozing from me, trickling slowly down my leg. I moved back to the step where we'd been, sitting again on that spot, staining the place with the juice of our bodies.

We never said goodbye. I never told him my time was up. The last day was like any other we'd had, no different in any way. He'd not been to the apartment, my time with him having been spent entirely in the sun. I'm sure he was a little disappointed when I didn't show up at the fountain, returning again to his friends beneath the trees, kicking a ball, watching out again for another tourist girl.

The night before I left, I washed my dress as usual, leaving it to dry on the balcony. Rising early that morning of leaving, up with the sun, out in the street. Not a sinner there. To that old church I went, in the old part of town. In my straw bag, the bag I'd bought there, was my white dress, sunglasses, shoes made of straw and hemp, the lot topped with the straw hat. The lot left on the steps of the church, like an abandoned child.

Technology came to my bedsit in the form of a clock-radio, my old clock having become unreliable. The clock-radio is cream in colour, with a red digital display which glows in the dark like the sacred heart lamp of old. I missed the tick of the old clock, never noticing it was there until it was gone. The initial fascination with the new clock was in watching the numbers change, my eyes fixed on the display like one watching television, while the initial shock was in discovering the exactness of the order in which I passed my days. The notion that I went to bed in or around half-past eleven was replaced with the knowledge that I was getting into bed most nights at 23:23. Coming in the door from work was then 17:08, not ten past five or so; waking from my Saturday morning lie-in became 10:33 as opposed to half-past ten or thereabouts. Time had become so exact.

I discovered that the numbers of the display are made up of individual bars of light, all numbers developing from seven bars of light which have the shape of the digital number eight. Number one is the darkest number, having only two bars of light, next is number seven with three, followed by four which has four, then number two, three and five have five, while zero, six and nine have six bars, number eight lights up all seven bars, making it the brightest.

Of the double-digit hour numbers, number twenty is the brightest of these, lighting up eleven bars of light between the number two and zero, the darkest of the double-digit hour numbers is, as you would expect, eleven.

The brightest of the seconds double-digits are twenty-eight, thirty-eight and fifty-eight – the moments brighter than the hours, naturally; the darkest being the same as the darkest hour number.

So the brightest moments in the day are in that half hour, or so, before midnight, two minutes to midnight being the last of those moments, 23:58, on the eve of a brand new day, so many possibilities, so much that could actually happen, so much to be left behind, the room brightening to the glow of the display.

I first noticed the varying degree of brightness generating from the display on seeing how dull it became at eleven minutes past one, 1:11, the darkest time of the day, a dark hour for anyone waiting for sleep, oblivion, a dark hour for anyone planning a tomorrow which would be no different from the day after or the one before, a sad hour to be alone, listening to the world having fun.

Pedro is not Leo's father.

Leo was born three years after that holiday, and if anyone had told me then that I would ever have a child, I would have been amused, intrigued to know how, why I would have allowed such a development in my life. He was born in 1990.

It was a question of age, but not my age; instead the age

of my mother intrigued me, her age when she gave birth to me. Thirty-three she was, the same age as Jesus when they crucified him on a hill called Calvary.

I do not know the date of my mother's birthday, only her death-day, so I can't be entirely sure she had actually reached her thirty-third birthday when I was born; all I have to go on is: fourteen from forty-seven equals thirty-three.

I was thirty-two, catching up with my mother, soon to be the age she was when she had me.

Was she in love with him at thirty-two? or desiring to have and to hold a child of her own at thirty-two? or more intent on leaving her father's house at thirty-two? – a man before her, a man behind her.

I was not in love, nor really desiring a child, and had long since left my father's house: a woman alone, pondering her time when young, the child mother to the woman.

That thinking of age, mine and how soon I would be the age my mother was when she had me, caused me to wonder, long sessions of wonder, sitting up in bed, staring into my darkened room, late into the night. During those dark hours I began to see a different shape for my life, began to recognise my choice, for better or for worse.

Curfew. Decent women, those, for instance, who wouldn't be caught dead alone in a pub, live under a curfew. A café curfew. As soon as it's six, café closing time, it's time for all decent, unpartnered women to be off the streets, no room for them in the bright lights of burger world, to re-emerge in twos and threes, but not alone, and if alone, then to be on their way to someone.

A man alone, decent or otherwise, can be on his way to some place, can stand at a bar, alone, and watch, while we chatter together, posing, rivals for the romance, much decided in the length of a look.

I did not have the courage to brave, alone, the world of the dance, could not see myself waiting to be chosen, saying yes to the dance but yet not knowing, passing from one set of arms to another, exchanging names and small-talk and meaningful glances, taken to his place, or by a wall, or not taken at all, then to brave, again, the game of the dance.

When I looked through the open window of the car, seeing an eager, male face, I nodded, stepped forward and opened the door.

From the time of my first late-night walks beneath the trees which flanked the park's railings, getting for myself a flavour of something that once gave joy, I had known the area was a pick-up spot for prostitutes. I had learned to avert my head as cars crawled by, never looking in the faces of men walking towards me.

I still have the money from that night: well-used notes buried beneath those photos in that white shoebox.